D0122235

SILENT THUNDER

LOREN D. ESTLEMAN

SILENT
THUNDER

An Amos Walker Mystery

HOUGHTON MIFFLIN COMPANY

BOSTON 1989

For information about permission to reproduce selections from
this book, write to Permissions, Houghton Mifflin Company,
2 Park Street, Boston, Massachusetts 02108.

Library of Congress Cataloging-in-Publication Data

Estleman, Loren D.
Silent thunder / Loren D. Estleman.
p.   cm.
"An Amos Walker mystery."
ISBN 0-395-41075-4
I. Title.
PS3555.S84S55   1989   88-32295
813'.54 — dc19   CIP

Printed in the United States of America

Q 10 9 8 7 6 5 4 3 2 1

To Irene Estleman
and to the memory of
Randolph "Red" Estleman,
my aunt and uncle

$$=\!\!=\!1\!=\!\!=$$

ERNEST KRELL LOATHED WINDOWS. The warehouse on the Detroit River that he had converted into offices with his wife's money didn't have any, and the house the Krells shared in Bloomfield Hills, a large brick splitlevel with an acre of slick lawn and decorative shrubbery masking the broken glass atop the brick wall that encircled it, was equipped with those tricky amber panels that allow light in but won't let you see inside or out. Every journalist who had ever written him up in *Detroit Monthly* and *Guns and Ammo* had hauled out his vest-pocket Freud to explain the aversion, but the plain fact was Krell had been with the United States Secret Service for seventeen years and had grown tired of warning people away from windows.

I rang his doorbell on the first lush day of summer. You know the one: You go to bed with rain rattling against the siding and when you get up, the trees are fat with leaves and the sky is so blue it hurts your eyes. The birds are in good voice, the breeze is like a lover's breath on your cheek, and even in the city, under the soft asphalt and sweet auto exhaust, you can smell fresh-cut grass. It's always a weekday, when you have to go to work.

The door was opened by a small mouse-faced woman with short brown hair curling all over and graying at the roots. Her dress was just a dress and the clear buttons in her ears were just something to keep the holes from closing. She wore no make-up.

"Are you Mr. Walker?" Her mouth was arranged in one of those fevered smiles that look as if their owners expect to have them slapped off their faces at any moment.

I said I was.

"I'm Mrs. Krell. Ernest is waiting. Please come in."

I followed the slightly stooping Mrs. Krell down two carpeted steps into a large sunken room with a stone fireplace the size of my garage. The walls were done in burled walnut and a carpet with an Oriental design lay on the floor on a pad as thick as a gym mat. Over the mantel hung an oil portrait in a baroque frame of Ernest Krell at twenty in an army lieutenant's uniform, painted just about the time he had been wounded in Korea. He had a pale face and very black hair cropped too close and stood with one booted foot propped up on a leather dispatch case. His eyes were as blue as eyes get anywhere.

"You're late. The woman will be here any minute."

I blinked, as anyone would when addressed by a picture. "Sorry," I said. "I thought you'd prefer me dressed. You called me at ten to seven."

It wasn't the picture, of course. Across from it, like an image in a clouded mirror, stood its subject, forty years older in everything but hair color. The hair was a little longer now and not as thick, but every bit as black, and suspiciously so. His face was still pale but creased at the eyes and from the nose to the mouth, the way faces become when their owners spend seventeen years scanning the rooftops for snipers. A big man — he went six-three and two hundred — he had on a black suit with lavender fleurs-de-lis to soften its starkness and a magenta tie held in place with a steel clasp. Scuttlebutt said he had had the clasp made from the shrapnel that had gone into his hip in Pusan.

There was a pause while he waited for me to come forward and shake hands and I wasn't going to do it. "Well, sit down," he said then. "I want to brief you before Mrs. Thayer arrives."

I took a seat on a soft leather sofa the color of gray chalk. Mrs. Krell, who had disappeared, returned while I was crossing my legs and placed a saucer containing four lemon cookies on the glass coffee table. That was a disappointment. I'd gotten home too late to eat supper the night before and had missed breakfast.

"Coffee, Mr. Walker? I'm afraid decaffeinated is all we have. Ernest's doctor —"

"Decaffeinated will be fine, Esther. I'm sure Mr. Walker isn't interested in hearing about my medical condition."

When she had left, I said, "Who's Mrs. Thayer?"

"In a moment. How long have you been working with Reliance now?"

"Eight years off and on. Whenever things get slow down my street."

"All that time, and you haven't been offered a permanent position?"

"It's been offered."

"Oh." He went over to the fireplace, where the sunlight filtering in through one of the panels made his black hair and white skin look more painted than the painting, and spent some time studying Lieutenant j.g. Krell. "I built Reliance out of nothing. When I came to this city, people who needed an investigator had to depend on filthy little hacks who worked out of the backs of tattoo parlors. They'd as soon strike a deal with the party you wanted investigated as with you. I introduced integrity and science."

"They do go hand in hand," I said. "Like bread dough and bicycles."

He ignored the comment, if indeed he'd heard it, which he probably had; it's always a mistake to confuse pomposity with density. "Reliance now has two hundred operatives in four states," he said. "They trace everything from computer fraud to threats endangering the national security. We almost never have to go outside the organization to satisfy a client's needs."

"I live on 'almost.' Also cookies." When Mrs. Krell came with the coffee I ate one and washed it down with the castrated liquid. The cookie tasted like the label from a bottle of ReaLemon.

"Thank you, Esther. When Mrs. Thayer comes, have her wait in the foyer."

She went out. I had started to think it was the maid's day off, but the way Krell's requests sounded like orders and the way Mrs. Krell obeyed them without comment said that no professional menial had ever set foot inside the household's three thousand square feet. The uninitiated would have been hard put to guess which was the retired civil servant and which the last survivor of the great industrial family that had invented the carburetor. The frequency with which the Ernests of this world latch on to the Esthers is one for Darwin.

"Who's Mrs. Thayer?" I asked.

He stopped looking at the portrait and looked at me. Either the artist had gotten carried away with blue or Krell's eyes had faded in four decades, to a zinc gray. "I spent yesterday going through the records, Walker. You've done the agency some favors. I deplore the way you operate, of course; but I suppose every grand army must have its Marshal Ney, charging the guns again and again and having his horse shot out from under him every time."

"I don't guess the horses approve either. Who's Mrs. Thayer?"

"A woman who shot her husband to death."

"Oh. *That* Mrs. Thayer."

"You know the case?"

"Just what they told in the papers."

The *News* and *Free Press* had been full of it for a while, and the national tabloids still were, despite a request by the attorneys involved to avoid trying the defendant in the media. Constance Thayer, after a night of clubbing, drugs, and alcohol, had seized an automatic pistol from the collection of husband Doyle Thayer Jr. and emptied it into his back as he lay naked and unconscious on his stomach in the bedroom of their Iroquois Heights home. The drugs and charges of wife-beating, together with the fact that Thayer was the heir to Thayer Industries, which specialized in the manufacture of the fuel solenoid that went into every recreational vehicle made in the United States, had kept the story fresh for weeks, and when it began to fade, the news that Constance Thayer had appeared in triple-X films before she met Doyle had breathed new life into it for another month. Depending upon who was telling it, she was either an abused woman pushed beyond endurance or a gold-digging slut who had seized her opportunity to inherit millions.

"Mrs. Thayer's attorneys have engaged Reliance to investigate her late husband's affairs," Krell said. "They feel that when the truth comes out about what kind of man he was, she'll be acquitted on grounds of justifiable homicide, if not out-and-out self-defense."

"Like he didn't wear pajamas, so he deserved to eat lead?"

"Like he was a monster who enjoyed degrading his wife in public and private as a vacation from his dealings with pushers and traffickers in contraband weapons. Like if she didn't stop him when she did, it could be Doyle Thayer Junior facing the charge of beating his wife to death, and likely getting off because of his father's influence. I thought you fancied yourself a protector of the weak."

"She seems to have done a pretty decent job of protecting

herself. And a private gun collection doesn't make Thayer Muammar Qaddafi."

Krell's brows — they were black, like his hair — went up. "You haven't heard? I suppose they are keeping it under wraps. Still, it's difficult to explain away all those crates they've been removing from Thayer's basement."

"Crates?" I helped myself to another cookie.

"As of yesterday — and they're still counting — agents from the FBI and the Bureau of Alcohol, Tobacco, and Firearms had carried away from that mansion the largest number of illegal munitions ever seized from a private citizen. The man had everything from light assault rifles to howitzers. They're still emptying the place."

"Was he expecting trouble?"

"Only from his insurance company. Give some people money without their having to work for it and they're bound to spend it on all kinds of outlandish toys." He leaned against the mantel of the fireplace of the house he had built with his wife's inheritance.

I wanted a cigarette, but I remembered Krell didn't allow smoking around him. Instead I crossed my legs the other way. "Sounds like the Feds've done half the job. Why call me?"

"I forgot. You're the man who asks why." He touched his tie clasp. "There are certain disadvantages to being big, as I'm sure the government men assigned to the case are learning. When you have a hundred people working on something, everyone knows you're involved and goes underground; but you *need* a hundred people to trace the origins of an arsenal as large as Thayer Junior's. That's not what I'm interested in. All I want to do is gather enough dirt on him to make my client look clean by comparison. If I'm going to do that, I can't afford to stampede the scum he dealt with when it gets out Reliance is investigating his associations."

"I get it. You want a ground mole."

"Does that offend you?"

"I'd be in the wrong business if it did. I just wanted to hear you say it."

"We'll pay two thousand a week, first week in advance. Can you start immediately?"

"I haven't said I'll take the job."

"Well?"

"I don't know yet."

He came away from the fireplace and stuck his hands in his pockets. He didn't look even a little like Lincoln. "Your opinion of Reliance and the way I run it is no secret. I could tell you what I think about dog-and-pony shows like yours, but there wouldn't be any point in it. We need each other from time to time."

"No argument."

"So why are you being coy?"

I drank coffee in place of the third cookie I wanted; which was a placebo for the smoke I really wanted. There were only two left in the dish, with another guest coming. "I'm as coy as a breed bull, Mr. Krell. I just want to meet the lady before I commit myself. For all I know she may have shot her husband because there wasn't an axe handy."

"Dear me. If lawyers felt as you do, the prison population would outnumber civilians ten to one."

"If we're talking about the Wayne County Jail, I think it already does." My cup came up empty. As there didn't seem to be any refills coming I returned it and the saucer to the table. "I don't own much. One house, a couple of suits, a partnership with my bank in a two-year-old Chevy. And a big fat illusion about myself that I'd hate to lose. I want to meet the lady."

"I see," he said, sounding like he didn't.

We were looking at each other when the doorbell rang. It works that way sometimes, even outside of novels.

=2=

AT KRELL'S REQUEST Mrs. Krell brought her in a few moments later, and nobody ever looked less like Lizzie Borden. She went medium height and not much past a hundred and ten in a tailored pink suit with a grayish cast — ashes of rose, I think they call it — over a blue silk blouse, the jacket pinched at the waist. Her hair was of that shade that can't decide to stay blond or throw away caution and go red. She had a tan she hadn't gotten in jail and hazel eyes, if eye color means anything in this time of tinted contact lenses. The thin chain around her neck was gold and from what I could see it was the only jewelry she wore. She looked Irish.

"Constance Thayer, Amos Walker," Krell said.

She lent me her hand long enough to feel coolness and an instant of pressure, then called it in. Her perfume reminded me of wildflowers growing on the other side of a hill.

"Mr. Krell told me you're a capable detective," she said. Her voice was light, without a regional accent of any kind. "You look big enough to do the job."

"Not next to Mr. Krell."

Krell made a burring noise in his throat that passed for a chuckle. Large men always respond positively to comments about their size. "Let's sit down. Can Esther get you something? Coffee?"

"Some bourbon would be nice."

"Water? Ice? A mixer?" If a drink order at 9:00 A.M. surprised him, he didn't show it.

"A glass will do." She was looking at me when she said it, and I thought I saw something; but it was still early and I was out of my head with hunger. The lemon cookies had only made it worse.

I shared the sofa with Constance Thayer while Krell made easy work of filling the love seat adjacent. She opened her purse, a blue clutch the size of a poker chip. "May I smoke?"

Krell didn't pause five minutes. "If you must." He shoved an empty saucer at her.

I watched her pluck a cigarette out of a gold Pall Mall package and get it burning with a slim platinum lighter. Tipping her head back to inhale she exposed the long line of her throat. There were no creases in it. I counted her rings mentally and came up with thirty.

"Before we begin," Krell said, "and regardless of whether you decide to represent Reliance in Mrs. Thayer's behalf, I need your promise that everything that's said in this room will be held in absolute confidence."

" 'Courtesy, efficiency, confidentiality,' " I quoted.

He winced. "I'm considering changing that motto. It sounds old-fashioned."

"It always has been. And I made the promise when I agreed to come."

"Since technically you'll be working for Mrs. Thayer's counsel, the privilege is legal. Of course, you might cool your heels in jail forty-eight hours waiting for the judge to agree."

"It wouldn't be the first time. I've got two of the coldest heels in town."

"The Pirates' Oath," Constance Thayer said. "Pass the dead cat. He didn't move, you know."

I said, "He didn't?"

She shook her head minutely and used the saucer, although there weren't any ashes yet. "I guess I saw it on TV too many times. You see it so much there you get to think you've really seen it. I expected him to jerk or try to get up. Well, he did jerk the first time, but it might have been just the bed swaying under him. There wasn't that much blood. The bullets made little blue holes."

"I heard you were bunged up at the time," I said.

"Not so much I didn't know what I was doing. That's not the defense we're using. Leslie wanted to use it, but I said no, it wasn't true."

"Leslie?"

"Leslie Dorrance," Krell offered. "Mrs. Thayer's principal attorney."

"I read that. I just never heard anyone call him Leslie before. Not bad."

She looked at me, and there it was again. "Is that all you can say? Most people seem to want to genuflect whenever I mention him."

"He writes a lot of books and sells a lot of books and nobody seems to notice that most of his clients go to jail anyway. Maybe not for as long as if it was any other attorney, so I say not bad. Perry Mason spoiled my generation for the real legal profession."

"As a matter of fact, he is planning to write a book about this case. He had me sign a release when he offered his services. What's funny?"

She'd caught me grinning. "It's just that if I were up for murder I wouldn't think of it as 'this case.' "

"That's how long I've spent cooped up with lawyers lately. You start to talk like them."

"How soon before you shot him did Mr. Thayer beat you the last time?"

"An hour."

A little more smoke wouldn't hurt Krell further. I got out a Winston and was patting my pockets for matches when Constance Thayer lit it for me with the platinum lighter. I looked at her, but it wasn't there this time. She was just doing a fellow smoker a favor. "The law's clear on self-defense in this state," I said when she had put the lighter away. "There has to be immediate danger."

"Leslie hopes to establish a new precedent. It wasn't the first time Doyle worked me over, but it was one of the worst. Many more like it and he'd have killed me. I just didn't want him to hit me again." As she said it, I could see the bruises under her make-up. It didn't matter whether they were actually there. It was in the way she spoke about being hit; her voice lost its cushion. Mrs. Krell, who had brought her bourbon while she was speaking, set it down on the coffee table and withdrew without pausing. What spouses think of the things they overhear I couldn't begin to guess.

"What the press says about you doing dirty movies," I said. "Is that hype?"

"No, I made two of them when I was in college in California. I was brought up to believe sex was clean, a beautiful act. I couldn't see anything wrong with making tuition money out of it."

"Why'd you quit?"

"They never changed the sheets."

"The work takes a strong stomach. Walking away from it takes guts. I have to wonder why someone who could come out with her head still on would let herself get slapped around."

"In the end, of course, I wouldn't," she said. "But I see what you mean. All I can say is you didn't know Doyle. He was wonderful when he wasn't zonked, a beautiful creature with a sensitive soul."

"And a couple of million dollars' worth of U.S. Army ordnance in the basement."

"Everybody's interested in something. He was like a little boy whenever he got a new one. They weren't weapons to him at all, really. Just shiny baubles. I'll never forget the day he took delivery on the German eighty-eight." She smiled, remembering.

"Who was his connection?"

"I never knew. He'd get a call, and then I'd overhear him bargaining. He never used names."

"You never answered when a call came in?"

"Once. Doyle grabbed the receiver from my hand when I was asking the man his name. He had a Southern accent, that's all I remember. It was at least a year ago."

"Black?"

"I really couldn't say."

I made a note. I had my pad out now. "What about when Doyle took delivery? What kind of vehicle?"

"Different ones at different times. They came to the basement door. The smaller things like the pistols and rifles came in cars, and once an old beat-up pickup truck. They delivered the heavy stuff in one of those big trucks with a canvas top, like you see in National Guard convoys on the expressway. No," she added, before I could ask, "I never got any license numbers."

"You and your husband had a boy, I think. Would he remember anything?"

"Jack's away at school. I sent him. He's not going to be involved."

The way she said it, staring at me through the smoke from her cigarette, closed that street. "Where does Doyle Senior stand?" I asked.

"Foursquare in favor of reinstating the death penalty in Michigan. He had Doyle all primed to replace him as board chairman of Thayer Industries in a couple of years. Now he wants to get his hands on Jack. That will be a lot easier if I go away for murdering Jack's father."

The air was becoming thick with smoke and something else. Krell got up and slid open one of the light panels a few inches, letting in fresh air. "Leslie Dorrance has filed a motion for a change of venue," he said. "If there's a judge in the Detroit area that Doyle Thayer Senior hasn't played golf with, he doesn't play. You might want to look for a lot of heat from that quarter."

I felt myself relaxing. Krell's stated reason for throwing the case in my lap had been bothering me. Now I could concentrate on the interview.

"How's chances of getting the venue changed?" I asked.

Constance Thayer laughed shortly, not a pleasant sound. "That decision is made by a judge."

"What's the date for the preliminary hearing?"

"July thirty-first," Krell said. "We have three weeks."

"Short date." I was looking at the woman. "You make enemies with style."

That brought a brief smile. She took one last drag at the Pall Mall and squashed it out in the bottom of the saucer. "The thing about marrying money is you can't ever make a clean break, even by killing. If I'm found not guilty, I stand to inherit a third of Doyle Industries' stock. That puts me in partnership with Doyle's father."

"You could give it up," I said.

"No. No, I earned it. If I charged only ten dollars per black eye, I earned every penny. Also I want to have something to give Jack that he didn't get from his grandfather."

Krell was standing by the fireplace again. He liked to strike a pose with the portrait at his back. "What's your decision, Walker? If it's no I have to make some calls."

I smoked. "I'll take it."

Constance Thayer said, "May I ask why?"

"Two reasons," I said. "Well, three. I don't like seeing anyone get ganged up on, especially a woman who's been bounced around enough. And when you had a chance to cop a plea on grounds of diminished capacity you didn't, on account of it wasn't true. Anyone who'd do something that stupid has got to be telling the truth."

She smiled again. "And the third reason?"

"You don't want to just come out even. You want the cake and the box it came in. To me that says you've got the tickets not to change your mind a week before the hearing and plead guilty so that I've wasted two weeks."

"That's important to you?"

"A guy likes to think he's doing something more than ripping pages off calendars. One question."

"Why isn't Leslie here?"

I nodded. Her habit of reading thoughts took some getting used to.

"He's in New York, having lunch with his publisher. You haven't a publisher, have you, Mr. Walker?"

I shook my head, then added, "I read a book once."

"Cervantes?" She was enjoying the conversation.

"Blomberg. *So You Want to Be a Private Eye.* Third edition."

"When can you start?" Krell was not enjoying the conversation.

I flipped the pad shut, killed my cigarette, and got up. "I think I already did."

═3═

THE BOARD OF HEALTH had closed down the burger place near my building, after which a delicatessen had bustled in, scoured the griddle, and named all the sandwiches after well-known Detroiters. My favorite booth had been ripped out and replaced with three tables the size of golf tees. I claimed the least wobbly of the three, had the Tommy Hearns — two fried eggs beaten to a pulp, served on toasted canvas, and vastly overrated — and went to work.

It's an old building, but I like old buildings. There are few surprises. In my little water closet I could smoke a cigarette waiting for hot water to wheeze its way up the rusty pipes, and sitting at my desk I could tell by the chords the old boards in the hallway struck when someone passed over them if it was Rosekranz the super or the guy who sold aluminum doors over the telephone in the office next to mine or the man in the corner suite who only came in three times a week to collect his mail.

There had been changes. The building maintenance crew had paid its annual visit to my office, steam-cleaned the rug, and found a pattern. I had grown tired of looking at the framed original *Casablanca* poster across from my desk — Bogart's stare in my direction had taken on more than its usual contempt — hung it on a different wall, and put up in its place a print of the Remington Arms Company's painting of Custer's Last Fight. Every time I looked at it I hoped to see the tide turning in Custer's favor, but it hadn't so far. Apart from that the place was the same as it had been in every other year, from the furniture that had come with the door and windows to the view of the roof of the building next door to the butterflies on the wallpaper. I liked it fine. I had my name on the door and a fresh three-year lease in the safe with my change of shirts.

The mail was looking up. I had two checks from former clients, a fat package containing a reverse directory so I didn't have to depend on my contact in the fire department when I had a telephone number and no name to go with it, and a certificate that entitled me to one free lesson in forensics from a correspondence school in Kansas City. I put the checks in the safe, found room for the directory in the top drawer of the desk, crumpled the certificate from Kansas City, and caromed it off Custer's forehead straight into the metal wastebasket in the corner. A day that began with a job and no bills was better than most.

The buzzer sounded in the outer office. I waited, and when the knock came at the brain box I said it was open. In came a long stretch of black youth in gray sweatpants and a black tank top with RETURN OF THE EVIL DEAD silkscreened across the front in dripping red letters. He had a flattop and a gold ring in one ear. With a little grunt he plunked the stack of old newspapers he was carrying onto the desk. Dust skinned out from between the pages. "Them the ones you wanted, Mr. Walker?"

I leaned forward to check the dates. "Them are those. Ten do it?" I stopped sitting on my wallet and thumbed out a bill.

He thanked me, folded it lengthwise and sidewise, and poked it into the top of his sweats. He started to leave.

"Second, Marcus." He stopped. "How's things at the store?"

"Things is things."

"Ever miss Young Boys Incorporated?"

He smiled without showing teeth. "They never was no Young Boys, Mr. Walker. Well, maybe at the start, but by the time the TV and the papers heard the name and started using it, nobody else was. Same with Pony Down. What's to call a bunch of kids running shit? No, I don't miss it. 'Cept the money."

"Still clean?"

He held out his forearms and turned them over.

"Doesn't mean anything, Marcus. You always shot behind your knees."

"You want me to strip?"

"I'd rather pass. I've seen some ugly things in here, but that's one more than the landlord allows me."

He grinned then all the way up. "You wouldn't say that if you *seen* my knees."

I waved at him and he left. I had pulled Marcus out of a crack house on Sherman when I was looking for another woman's son, got him into a rehab program, and practiced a little creative extortion when he came out to snare him a job stacking cans in a party store two blocks from my building. Sometimes he scratched up old copies of the local papers from the back room for me, saving me a few hours in the Detroit Public Library. Every ten years or so I do something for someone who isn't a client, and while it never works out, all the precincts hadn't reported in yet on this one. I never found the son either.

I spent the morning following the Thayer killing through the papers and making notes. The *Free Press* ran the usual sidebars calling for stiffer handgun laws, the *News* made a case in favor of a get-tough-on-murder stance on the bench, and *USA Today* described the black taffeta shift Constance Thayer wore to her arraignment. One of the names connected with the story came as no surprise and I dialed a number at Detroit Police Headquarters. A woman whose voice I didn't recognize answered on the private line.

"Lieutenant Alderdyce, please," I said.

"You mean Inspector Alderdyce?"

I took my feet off the desk. "How come hell froze over and nobody called me?"

"The promotion came down last week. He's testifying in court today. This is Detective Deming. Perhaps I can help."

Another lady detective at 1300 Beaubien. It made me wonder again about the temperature down below. Aloud I said, "This is Amos Walker, a friend of John's. He was one of the Detroit people called in to help with the Doyle Thayer Junior homicide. I thought he could tell me the name of the federal agent in charge there now."

"I've heard your name." Her tone sounded less professionally cordial, if you can trust the telephones at headquarters. "The Thayer killing took place in Iroquois Heights. That's out of this jurisdiction."

"Detective Deming, you know and I know and everyone but the voters in Iroquois Heights knows the cops there couldn't tell a murder from a tufted titmouse. If you don't, their chief does, and that's why he called your chief."

"Even if he did, it's their case now. Certainly it isn't federal. What's *your* interest, Mr. Walker?"

I made some doodles in my pad. "The metro cops wouldn't hear anything about the Feds clearing several hundred long tons of military arms out of a private house ten miles from Detroit, huh."

"I didn't say that. But I'd be interested in where *you* heard it."

"Don't tell me. John Alderdyce approved your promotion from Records."

"Traffic. Good-bye, Mr. Walker. Remember, we're only a phone call away." This one had a way of hanging up delicately that was worth any sweaty male sergeant's slam-dunk in my face.

Cops. Way back when, I had entertained the idea that the women would change things downtown, but when you mix fresh water with salt you still can't drink it.

Iroquois Heights was growing; noxious weeds generally do little else. It had a brand-new school, construction had begun on a civic center to incorporate all the city offices under one roof for the first time, and there was the usual talk of building a domed stadium where a dozen sports could be played indoors on artificial turf. Athletes of the future will be known by their silver skins and white eyes, like aquatic lizards that spend their entire lives in subterranean pools and never see sunlight. The well-heeled local citizenry, who had fled Detroit to avoid having their skulls cracked open and their pockets picked, would be emptying their wallets for that project for years to come, and the mayor and the city council wouldn't even have to raise a lead pipe.

The Thayer home was a large brick colonial occupying four acres at the end of a cul-de-sac, surrounded by great oaks planted in martial rows and black with shade. That was as much of it as I saw, because a seven-ton truck with a square silver grille blocked the entrance to the street facing out. Its box took up the entire street.

I parked against the curb, got out, and waited, smoking, with my back against the Chevy's roof. If what Krell and Mrs. Thayer had told me was true and it wasn't just someone moving into or out of the neighborhood, I wouldn't have to wait long. In any case the day was warm and I could do worse than lean there listening to a squirrel perched high in one of the oaks chattering angrily at the big metal thing spoiling its view of the acorns below.

After a couple of minutes a young man in a brown leather jacket and jeans came my way along the sidewalk in front of the Thayer house. They had progressed from the old days of Robert Hall suits and skinny ties, but they hadn't gotten it right just yet; the jacket was brand new and the jeans were pressed. His hair was black and fashionably long, although long wasn't the fashion that season. And no one but a Fed strolls quite that way, as if he's got no place to be and all the time in eternity to get there.

"Hi," he said, when he got within earshot. "Are you looking for an address?"

"Thanks, I found it."

He scratched his ear. It stuck out a little, even under the hair. If he cut it short the way they were wearing it now he'd have looked like Norman Rockwell's favorite PFC. He said, "I think it must be the wrong one."

Behind him, the truck lurched on its springs, as if something heavy had been lifted into the box. He didn't flinch or offer any other indication that he was aware of it, I had to hand him that. They're calling it "plausible deniability" in Washington now. If Noah Webster were alive he'd commit suicide with a rusty infinitive.

"Who's quarterbacking today?" I asked.

"Quarterbacking?"

"Calling the plays. Barking the show. Dealing the aces. Warping the speed. Beam me up, Scotty. I want to talk to your leader."

"I'm afraid you're a little out of your neighborhood."

"You said it, brother." I snapped away the butt and took out one of my cards. He made a little move toward his jacket while I was fishing for it, then scratched his shoulder when

I didn't haul a sawed-off out of my wallet. I hadn't thought anyone was still wearing those underarm rigs; in warm weather they're a little less comfortable than a chastity belt. I scribbled a name on the back of the card and held it out.

He took it and read both sides. "Is this supposed to mean something?"

"Not to you. Show it to your boss. I'll wait. Coffee? No, thanks, I just had lunch. It's sweet of you to ask."

I watched him study the choice. He was going to go on running the bluff. Then he wasn't. You can read these younger field men like a blackboard menu. He turned around and walked behind the truck.

When he came back he had someone with him, and this model was off the old line. He was a stout number with narrow lapels, a thin black tie on a white shirt through which I could make out the scoop neck of his undershirt, and a snapbrim hat whose brief brim had seen all of its snap. It was on the back of a big head of curly gray hair and under it was one of those rubber faces that you just know got that way by being rubbed a lot. He had a paunch and didn't care who knew it, and a smile with his mouth slightly open and no teeth showing. He was born too late to be played by Wallace Beery, which was a shame. He was carrying my card.

"Know this person well?" he asked me without preamble, waving it.

"Not very. I did a job for him a couple of years back."

"Official?"

"Personal."

"I'd like to know what it was."

"If you didn't, you wouldn't be worth a dime in the field."

He waited, not too long. Then he stuck out a big soft paw, which I took. "Horace Livingood, ATF. Want to see the ID?"

"Naw. Want to see mine?"

"What's the point? In this town they can stamp you a

bronze star while you're inside getting a tan. What can we do on you, Walker?"

"I'm working for Mrs. Thayer's attorney. I'd like to get a look at what you're carrying out of the basement. I already know some of it."

"That's classified," piped up the younger man.

"Excuse my rotten manners. This is Agent Pardo. He's new and thinks secrets should stay secret. I'm not so sure he's wrong."

"If you feel that way," I said, "you ought to camouflage the truck. Bounce it off a couple of dozen Edison poles, spray graffiti on it, and pile color TV sets and stereos in the back. They'd just think you were with the cops."

"I met some of them. Well, if this guy thinks you're straight up I guess I'd be an asshole not to."

I said nothing.

"Of course, you could be lying."

"I lie a lot," I concurred.

"I could call and verify." He rubbed his face with one hand, proving my guess right. Then he shook a Cigarillo out of a pack that had character and lit it with a Zippo. "Let somebody who hasn't got in his thirty do that. Those Washington switchboards are a pain in the ass."

Pardo said, "Mr. Livingood, I have to report this."

"You do that, Victor. Well, come take a look at the inventory. You'll think you died and went to Fort Dix."

He went back behind the truck. Agent Pardo and I followed.

Just like that.

4

THE HOUSE WAS ONE of the few in that section of Iroquois Heights without a fence or a wall to keep strangers out of the yard. It didn't need one. As we drew near the truck's open trailer, two men in blue government-issue Windbreakers came out of the walkout basement door carrying a clapboard crate with C-4 EXPLOSIVES stenciled on it in English, French, and Spanish. A dozen others were stacked inside the trailer. On the grass awaiting its turn for loading lay a .50-caliber machine gun with a perforated jacket, its disassembled tripod next to it.

Someone had pried two boards off the top of the crate. As it came past, Agent Livingood lifted something out of the inside and cradled it along his forearm. It looked like a Flit gun.

"Ever see one of these?"

"Pocket rocket," I said. "I carried them in Nam."

"Not like this one. Catch." He flipped it at me.

Reaching for it I damn near slapped it over the roof. It weighed less than a plastic toy.

"Not a speck of metal in it," he said. "Even the charge is C-4 plastic, enough to take out this side of the street once it's armed. You might as well send any old bazookas you've got lying around to the Smithsonian. You could carry this aboard any commercial airliner in the world in your overcoat pocket, walk right through those detectors that go off when a kid's braces pass through, and never hear a peep."

"Real progress. Next we'll be boarding them naked." I returned the weapon. It didn't look any more sinister than a skyrocket.

He stroked it. "What do you suppose a rich kid wants with a play-pretty like this?"

"Maybe when your old man's finished building everything up before you were born, knocking it down's all that's left. You want to put out that weed?" A length of ash from his Cigarillo had dropped onto the rocket's nose.

"Don't sweat it. This stuff's more stable than the currency." But he spat out the little cigar and squashed it underfoot.

"What's left inside?"

"Mr. Livingood." Pardo sounded like an assistant principal.

The older man ignored him. "Not much. Just the entire Albanian armory and an Afrika Korps armored halftrack. You said you're working for the wife?"

"Her lawyer."

"That twerp."

"You met him?"

"He tried to pump me about this operation, but he wouldn't let me question Mrs. Thayer about her husband's little arsenal. I told him to do what you might expect me to tell him to do. I'll be hearing from Washington about that any time now. Everybody's got friends in Washington but me. Funny, ain't it?"

"Hilarious."

"I don't mean that, I mean, all this heavy iron and the

rich little turd gets it the old-fashioned way, from his wife."

"I guess he couldn't get the howitzer upstairs."

"Oh, you heard about the howitzer?" His eyes were alive in the rubber face.

"I never heard of a secret that had a howitzer in it."

"Yeah." He lost interest again. He was one to watch. "This gun control stuff is a hoot. They ought to make everything legal, if you can prove you can clean it without shooting off too many toes."

"How many are too many?"

"Three." He was looking down at his feet.

"Where'd Thayer get it all?"

"Tell you when we finish inventorying it and run the serial numbers."

"When will that be?"

"Hell, I'll be two years into my pension. This asshole next to me will be Washington bureau chief by then."

Pardo said nothing.

"Spitball it," I said. "You don't look like someone who sleeps with the book."

"There's a book?" He grinned his baggy grin. Then he ran a hand over his face. "I don't find myself agreeing with Vic much. I never agree with Vic. But we've been working the local big iron dealers for two years and I'm just close enough to retirement not to want to blow it. Sorry."

I stepped on what felt like a pine cone and took my foot off it. It was a hand grenade, one of the old pineapples we used to practice with. Livingood noticed it, scooped it up with a grunt, and tossed it and the portable rocket launcher into the trailer.

"Mrs. Thayer told me an old beat-up pickup came to the basement door once," I said, when the hairs on the back of my neck lay down. "What do you hear from the Shooter?"

"Good old Shooter. I heard he married a rich divorcee and retired."

"You buy it?"

"He'll get out when they screw him into the ground. This is way out of his wheelhouse, though. Biggest thing he ever dealt was the MAC-10 he sold me, just before I busted him the last time."

"He tried to sell me a Thompson once."

"Did you see it?"

"The wrong end. The guy he was going to buy it from changed his mind and tried shooting up some cops with it."

"Blew him out from under his hat, I bet. Them old type-writers are too heavy and got a mean pull besides. Plus they jam. Any rookie with a crummy department-issue thirty-eight can plug you while you're still trying to clear the slide." His eyes flicked over my shoulder. "Here comes the law in Iroquois Heights."

I hadn't heard the big Pontiac coasting to a stop in front of the truck. It was robin's-egg blue, with the city seal etched in gold on the driver's door and the department's motto painted in matching italics on the rear fender.

" 'To serve and protect,' " Livingood read. "I wonder if the boys in Truth in Advertising know about that?"

A young officer in a uniform he had put on with a roller — it was the same color as the car, with a gold stripe on the pants — got out from behind the wheel and swaggered our way, sliding a walkie-talkie into a holder on his gun belt. Hatless, he wore his sandy hair in a crew with the temples shaved, gold-framed Ray-Bans with violet lenses, and a triangular moustache clipped with nail scissors and a slide rule. His gear, stowed in various loops and pockets of his belt and uniform, included a leather sap, a monkey stick, a pair of black jersey gloves with studded knuckles, two speed-loaders bristling with cartridges, and a Colt .357 Magnum with a fisted grip. His stomach was as flat as an inquisitor's rack.

"Good afternoon, Officer Pollard," said the senior agent.

"What can we do for you today and how much is it going to cost?"

Officer Pollard stopped in front of us and pointed a manicured finger at him. "That's showing disrespect for an officer in the performance of his duties. I could ticket you for that."

"Who's going to show you how to write it?"

Pollard made no answer to that. Up close, he wasn't as young as he appeared from a little distance; his spiky hair was going silver at the tips and the dark glasses couldn't hide the lines around his eyes. "The chief asked me to look in on you from time to time, find out if you needed anything."

"I know what he wanted you to find out."

Pardo spoke up. "Thank you, Officer. If we need anything, we'll let the chief know."

"Who's chief these days?" I asked.

The violet lenses turned my way slightly. "You're who?"

I showed him my ID. There was no telling if he was reading it. His lips didn't move, anyway.

"Uncle Sam buying private talent these days?" he asked when I'd put away my wallet.

"Just asking directions."

"Figured you were new or you'd know the chief's name is Proust."

"Deputy chief," I corrected. "An ex one at that."

"He's acting chief till the chief gets well, which he never will. And he ain't no ex."

"Impossible. He's under indictment."

"That don't mean he done it. Innocent till proven guilty, mister; that's how we do things in the U. S. of freaking A."

"Since when is Iroquois Heights in the U.S.A.?"

He jerked a thumb over his shoulder the way they teach in cop school. "You said you were asking directions, mister. The way out's that way."

He went back to his unit, wheeled it around, and lost some rubber going back the way he'd come. Livingood spat at the ground. "I heard they cleaned up this place," he said.

I said, "They used a dirty broom. You were telling me about Shooter."

"Was I?" He grinned. "Yeah, I guess I was. Last time I looked, he was doing business at the same old stand. You can try him. As far as the G's concerned, he's no bigger'n bait this season."

"What about Ma Chaney?"

"You do get around." He was interested again.

This time *I* grinned. "That's good, that tired civil servant number. How close are you to retirement really?"

"I don't expect to live to see it. You know Ma?"

"I did some business with her once out at the barn."

"She moved it. Not the barn, just what was inside. We don't know where yet. We can't get an undercover man past her. If her boys had half her smarts they wouldn't be in jails from here to Miami."

"That's all you can do for me?"

"If it's Christmas, where's the snow?"

I left him listening to Pardo, waited for the two men in Windbreakers to pass carrying a Chinese mortar, and got into my car, hoping a spark from the distributor wouldn't make a park out of that section of town.

It didn't, and I drove back to the office under a sky as blue as a nuclear warhead. I elbowed my way through the invisible customers lined up six deep in the reception room, got my little green book of dynamite out of the top drawer of the file cabinet, and dialed a number I had listed under a nifty code I had borrowed from a Marvel comic book. Waiting for an answer I watched Custer. It looked to me like he was holding his own.

On the twelfth ring a Mississippi accent answered. "So talk."

"Amos Walker," I said. "We've done business."

"Where?'"

"Parking lot on West Lafayette, about a year ago."

"I didn't axe when. What's my name?"

"Sonny boy."

He didn't laugh.

"Shooter," I said.

"Know why they call me that?"

"It sure isn't because you're always shooting your mouth off."

"They call me that 'cause I shoot square. You shoot square?"

"If all your customers shot square I'd be doing business with you over a glass counter in a store with bright lights and a window display."

"You a customer?"

"I could be, if you've got what I want."

"If you want it, I got it. If I ain't got it I can get it. If I can't get it, you don't want it. What do you want?"

"An interpreter."

Silence.

"Protection," I said.

"Buy a dog."

"I need more protection than that."

"Buy two dogs. You saying you want a *gun,* man?"

"I got guns. I want a case of C-4 plastic rocket launchers and a fifty-caliber machine gun."

"Going up after deer?"

I took another look at Custer. He seemed to be losing ground now. "You got what I want, or is what you said before just a stall? Because if it is I can report you to David Horowitz."

"Tell him take a number. I get back to you." I had a dead line.

Bright patter. The white noise of the grifter's world. I

hung up on the dial tone and checked the square of sunlight on the wall opposite the window. It looked high enough. I took my birthday bottle out of the deep drawer of the desk and floated some dust in a glass. Then I looked up Ma Chaney's number in the green book.

"Hello?"

Good old Ma. It was getting so almost nobody answered the telephone the old-fashioned way. I swallowed some antidote and used my name. "We met during that Virgil Boyd thing."

"I remember." Her voice was a cigarette wheeze without any inflection.

"I've got some questions to ask if you're not busy."

"Ma's never busy. Go ahead and ask."

"Not over the telephone. Where can we meet?"

"My house is in the same place it always was."

"When can I come out?"

"Ma's always home."

"How about five o'clock?"

"Bring money."

I barely had my hand off the receiver when the bell rang. It was Shooter.

"You know the warehouse district?" he asked.

"You mean Rivertown?"

"Screw Rivertown. That's an architect's drawing. I mean the warehouse district, railroad tracks and big ugly buildings with rats."

"Where in the warehouse district?"

"It don't matter, man. It ain't big enough to piss in since the mayor got his gold shovel. Five o'clock."

"Can't make it. How about four?"

"Four's fine. I be there at five." He did it to me again.

I called Ma back. "Something came up. Is four o'clock okay?"

"Ma takes her nap at four," said the owner of the wheezy voice.

"Six, then."

"At six I visit the hospital."

"I thought you never left home."

"Ma's got a boy in the hospital."

"How about tonight after seven?"

The wheeze turned into a short laugh that ended in a smoker's hack. "Ma works nights."

"I forgot. So when?"

"You come see Ma tomorrow anytime."

"Okay."

"Except six," she added.

I said okay again and wrote the appointment on my crowded social calendar, right between Shooter and the day I stay home and rotate my socks.

5

EVERY CASE NEEDS a place to start, a thread you can pull or an edge of tape you can get your thumbnail under. It was a long haul from your local Saturday Night Special dealer to the people who trafficked in plastic weapons the FAA hadn't heard about, but Constance Thayer's short court date didn't leave enough time to place an ad in *Soldier of Fortune*. I went home at four, shaved for the second time that day, and put on my good blue suit and a solid red tie over a white shirt fresh out of tissue and plastic: that clean-cut look and subliminal American flag that tells the world you're out to blow Russia right out of the *National Geographic*. I unscrewed the cap from a bottle of Brut and hesitated, wondering if it was a touch too much. Then I slapped it on. Subtlety was lost on the culture I was about to enter.

The old Detroit, the city of growling trumpets, window-tapping hookers, and contraband Canadian whisky served in smoky cellars, is still visible if you care to look for it and the mayor's contractors haven't gotten to it yet. At the moment they were busy ripping out the turn-of-the-century brick warehouses along the river and replacing them with hotels and office buildings that looked like Coke bottles, but they weren't quite finished. A hand-towel–size section along Jefferson still contained blackened box-shaped structures with painted-over windows standing on broken pavement. Disused rails twisted among heaps of rubble and old wooden pallets in one of the last places in the city that didn't stink of committee planning. Where do all the shattered people go when ugliness has been banished?

I parked next to a loading dock and waited with the windows down. Mine was the only vehicle in the area and I was the only thing breathing in it that I could see. The air smelled of concrete dust and worm-eaten oak and spilled sweat. Gusts off the river skinned the top layer of grit off the scenery and spread a gray mulch over my upholstery. To my right, at the end of a narrow passage two blocks long lined with dirty-faced buildings, the slick blue base of the Renaissance Center was just visible, like a prom queen among the lepers.

At five o'clock on the button a green Dodge club cab as old as unleaded gas came chugging down the alley and stopped a hundred yards away, where it was enveloped momentarily by its own plume of dust and burned oil. Its horn beeped. I got out and strode that way.

The man behind the wheel of the pickup cranked down his window and looked me over with heavy-lidded eyes in a face the color of blue coal. Chill air and loud music came out of the opening.

"You him?" The Mississippi was strong this evening.

"I'm me," I said.

"I don't remember faces, just guns. Get in." He closed the window and unlocked the door on the passenger's side.

The temperature was at least a dozen degrees cooler inside. The upholstery was maroon plush and the dash was padded leather with more gauges and dials in it than the cockpit of a DC-10. He had a sound system made in heaven and assembled in Tokyo that was belting out Fleetwood Mac loud enough to wake Jimmy Hoffa. I found the power cutoff and punched it. Silence hit me like a skillet.

"You don't like music?" he said.

"Not enough to sacrifice the fillings in my molars."

He showed me his own molars. Shooter was a long trickle of water whose bones showed under his skin in a tank top and striped shorts and alligator shoes without socks. He'd told me once he was allergic to leather and canvas. "What you packing?"

I opened my coat to show I was unarmed. He parked the copy of the *Shotgun News* he'd had in his lap over his sun visor and laid the nine-millimeter Beretta it had been hiding on top of the dash.

"You got to cover your ass in this work," he explained. "They found one of my old partners washing around a pier at the Detroit Yacht Club last week."

"They let him in?"

"Just his top half. That's all they found. Say, what you want to mess around with one of them big old water-cooled machine guns, anyway? I can put a Russian assault rifle in your hands for sixteen-fifty; weighs one-tenth as much and it's a whole hell of a lot more accurate."

"Where'd you get it, Afghanistan?"

I saw his molars again. "Man, these ain't rare books I'm dealing. You don't need to know where they come from."

"What about the big machine gun?"

"Oh, I can get it. Them plastic rocket launchers, now; I ain't ever seen one."

"Who has?"

"What am I, a Spiegel catalogue? Do your own shopping. You want the machine gun or not? It'll run you two grand."

I held up a hundred-dollar bill.

He started sweating and licked his lips. He shook and panted and walked up his side of the cab and across the ceiling and down my side, where he sat up in my lap and begged. Mostly, though, he stayed where he was behind the wheel and made no reaction at all. "You want change?"

"Uh-uh. Answers."

"Hold out your hand."

"Why?"

"I ain't going to put no shitty stick in it. Just hold it out."

I stuck out the hand without the bill in it. He made an impatient noise and turned it over so that the palm was up. He slipped two rings off his left hand and put them in it. He did the same with the three he was wearing on his right hand and unwound the gold chain from around his neck and added it to the pile. Finally he unplugged a diamond I hadn't noticed from his left earlobe and placed it on top. The hand was getting hard to hold up.

"That's fifteen thousand," he said. "I dressed light today on account of it's hot. I wipe my ass on C-notes."

"Well, for the next time you take advantage of the two-for-one fajita special at Carlos Murphy's." I waved it.

"You don't understand, man. Wait."

He pulled up his tank top. There was no ruby in his navel, which disappointed me a little. What there was was an old scar angling jaggedly up from below the waistband of his shorts to the arch of his rib cage, grub-white against the bluish black of his skin. It was puckered on the edges where the stitches had been pulled out.

I said, "Did you hurt yourself?"

"In a way I did. I made a mistake when I was new. I sold a gun to a man and when he asked who I bought it from I told him. Turned out the man was the Man. I got twenny-six months in Cassidy Lake for possession and attempted sale of stolen property, but the man I bought it from pulled five to fifteen years in Milan for burglarizing the National Guard Armory in Grayling. A friend of his talked to me in the handball court at Cassidy. He did his talking with a linoleum knife."

"That must've smarted."

"Didn't hurt at all, at the time. Two guys held me and he

just kind of slid it up my belly. The skin opened up like a fucking theater curtain and I watched my guts dump out. The croaker in the infirmary let me wait while he was taking care of a dozen cases of food poisoning from last night's haddock; he didn't figure I was worth wasting time on. It hurt later, but what I remember most is watching my skin open up and them blue guts flopping out." He tugged down the tank top and took back his jewelry.

"So what about the hundred?" I asked.

When he finished putting on the rings and chain he hit the power button and sat back, closing his eyes. The music came on full blast. I could feel the truck's old frame buzzing. I punched for silence.

"I'm not asking where you got any of the stuff you're dealing. I just want to know who's peddling military ordnance locally. I don't care if he's selling neutron bombs to minors. Let the Feds worry about that. I've got a client."

"Not for no hundred."

"How much?"

"What's your guts worth to you?" he asked.

"Don't go Saint Joan on me, Shooter. You haven't got the wardrobe."

"For two grand I could buy it."

I turned on the music, held up a palm, and reached for the door handle. This time he cut the power.

"Okay, eighteen. Nine hunnert to start."

"Five," I said. "The first hundred now. But it's got to turn into something."

"Fifteen. Half and half. No guarantees, man."

"Four hundred."

"That ain't how it *works*," he whined.

I scooped the Beretta off the dash before he could move and kicked out the magazine. I heeled it back in and ran back the action. "Empty." I tossed it into his lap. He gasped.

"Watch the *oysters*, man. Loaded pieces scare the shit out of me." He laid it on the seat. "A grand."

I got out my wallet and emptied it. "Two hundred's all I got on me."

"That's cool." He plucked the bills and the original hundred out of my hand. "I call you when it's set. We go see the man together. You better bring some for him too."

"You know my home number."

"You bet. You just sit there by that old telephone, wait for Shooter to call."

I snatched hold of his gold chain and gathered it in my fist. He said, "Grrrk!"

"Twenty-four hours," I said. "Then I come back and find out if your guts really are blue."

He nodded.

I let go and hit the button on the dash. A band that would have a name like Painful Rectal Itch shrieked at me about the joys of having nails driven through one's tongue.

"Do yourself a big one, Shooter. Spend the money on a good hearing aid."

"What?"

I shouted good-bye.

Quitting time. I'd planned on stopping for supper, but I was out of cash and I'd left all my credit cards in my other pants along with my Millionaires Club key and the diploma from Harvard. Instead I battered my way home through rush-hour traffic and around a pair of lady cops who were busy tying knots in the intersections. I didn't even have to smoke; I just rolled down the window and inhaled bus exhaust. By the time I swung into my driveway I had sweated through the white shirt and the knot of the red tie was down around my ankles.

I did it up, though, because a burgundy BMW was parked in front of my garage. Before I got out, I opened the glove compartment, racked a shell into the chamber of my unlicensed Luger, and stuck it under my belt. I couldn't remember entering any contests lately.

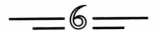

THE ANGLE OF THE SUN blanked out the car's windows so I couldn't see inside. I went up to the driver's side, where my body blocked the light and I could tell that someone was sitting behind the wheel. Whoever it was didn't move as I approached. I drew the Luger and tapped the butt against the glass. Going heeled always brings out my flair for the dramatic.

Theater was satisfied. The man, who had been dozing, opened his eyes, saw the automatic, and gave up the color in his face. It was a handsome face if you were a mare, with a five o'clock shadow worse than mine, black, comma-shaped brows, and topped by a retreating hairline that had left a patch of black widow's peak behind in its rout.

I did the border spin for effect, ending up with the butt in my palm, and made a cranking motion with my free hand. He had to start the engine to open the electric window.

"Mr. Walker?"

Exhaling, I took the hammer off cock and returned the Luger to my belt. "Sorry. The neighborhood's not what it was. Nice cars don't always mean nice people."

"You know who I am?"

"I've seen you on talk shows, Mr. Dorrance. I didn't think famous lawyers drove their own cars."

"I leased this one locally. I get most of my thinking done at the wheel." He'd composed himself quickly, a big talent with courtroom attorneys. "I was at your office a little while ago, but you were out. I thought you'd gone home. Nobody told me things got this hot here in the summer."

"Give it three months."

"Of course, it gets a lot hotter in Boston than a lot of people think. Have you been to Boston?"

"I trailed a bail-jumper there one winter. It can get cold there too." I glued a cigarette to my lower lip. "Let's go inside where we won't have to talk about geography and the weather."

"Do you have air conditioning?"

"I call it a window."

I opened his door for him. He was shorter than he appeared on television, although not short, and he was in his shirtsleeves with his tie loosened. They were expensive sleeves, too wrinkled to be anything but pure cotton, and the tie, slate-colored silk with a foulard pattern, would go at least seventy-five. He wore soft black loafers with tassels and thick soles, designed for standing for hours making impassioned speeches to juries. The maroon leather briefcase that a legal hawk like Dorrance would have lay on the passenger's seat in front.

He said nothing about my living room, but his coffee-colored eyes took in everything, from the clock that was not quite antique to my one good easy chair and the other sticks of furniture that had outlasted my marriage. Except for the clock I could walk away from all of it tomorrow without a last look. I opened the famous window and offered him a drink.

"Thanks, I don't. If you could spare a glass of water."

In the kitchen I cracked some ice, ran the tap into a tumbler tinted amber to disguise the Detroit in the local water, and mixed Ten High and Vernor's for myself. I found him looking over my little library on the shelf over the television set.

"Good books," he said, accepting the tumbler. "And read, from the looks of them. I work with private investigators frequently. Not many of them read."

"I'm not like other investigators. I was abandoned by wolves as a child and raised by my father."

"He was without education, I gather. Those who have had it take it for granted in their children."

I let that wander and indicated the easy chair. I started to sit down on the sofa, paused, took the Luger out of my waistband, put it on the end table, and lowered myself the rest of the way, avoiding the weak spring. I knocked the head off my highball. "Let's lose the small talk and get on with the firing, Mr. Dorrance."

He spent some time arranging the crease on his trousers before crossing his legs. "You've heard from Mrs. Thayer?"

"Not since this morning when I took the job."

"I must be losing my poker face, then."

"You can play poker for me anytime, Mr. Dorrance. You're not the only lawyer who works with private investigators. I knew before I left Ernest Krell's house we'd have this meeting."

"Really. I didn't."

"That's because you didn't know what he was up to. You're not stupid. Just because you spend a lot of time polishing your public image doesn't mean you've forgotten what put you where you are. This is a big case, a headline maker. You wouldn't have let any such meeting take place

without your presence if you'd known about it. Krell over-
stepped himself in going outside the agency without consulting you. He does that sometimes. He's not a detective
himself and doesn't understand there are rules to these
things."

"If you suspected that, why did you accept the case?"

"First why don't you tell me why you don't want me on it."

He set down his water untasted. He'd never intended to
drink any of it; taking it in the first place was one of the
rules I'd been talking about.

"I'm painting a picture with the help of the media," he
said. "The public must be made to view Constance Thayer
a certain way. A thing like that requires teamwork. I can't
afford to have an independent operator running around
stirring up dust. It blurs the picture."

"Sounds like you're working on creating a jury in your
own image," I said. "Isn't it your job to see the case never
gets beyond the preliminary hearing?"

"Everybody who ever watched Perry Mason thinks he
knows what my job is. Let's just say I play better when my
bow has two strings."

"Mumbo jumbo. I'm not the Bloomfield Hills Wednesday
Afternoon Ladies' Social and Current Events Society."

"I guessed that. I'll be more specific." He drew a flat
leather wallet from his shirt pocket and removed a pale
green rectangle of paper. "This is a cashier's check for
twelve hundred dollars. I think it's adequate compensation
for your time."

"I agreed to two thousand dollars a week. I've only been
on the case half a day."

"Consider it good faith money. I may have use for your
services someday."

"Hold out your hand, Mr. Dorrance."

"What?"

I took off my watch and extended it. He hesitated, then

took it. Before he could withdraw his hand I got out my wallet and slapped it on top of the watch. Then I sat back.

"I don't understand." He stared at the items.

"The watch cost twenty-five bucks when I bought it two years ago," I said. "I replaced the battery last month. The wallet's empty, but I've only had it a few weeks and you could probably get a buck for it at a junk store. I got this suit for a hundred. The tie cost four-fifty, that's dollars and cents. Put all of that together with everything you see in this room and you might come up with eight hundred bucks. The house is worth thirty thousand, although I'd be lucky to get twenty because of the neighborhood. I've got six hundred in the bank and I owe five more payments on the car. All told I'm worth about twenty-five grand, twice that much if I die because of my G.I. insurance, which goes to my ex-wife on account of I've never gotten around to taking her name off the policy. Do you really think a few hours of my time comes to twelve hundred dollars?"

"I see. Very colorful."

"Not even original. I stole it from a gun broker just today." I took back my watch and wallet.

"Do you want the check or not?"

"Mr. Dorrance, you weren't listening."

He put it away. "Payment or not, you're off the case. Krell was on my retainer when he hired you."

"Who's arguing?" I had some more whiskey and ginger ale. "What strategy are you using in court?"

His smile was bit-tight in the horse face. "It would hardly be ethical for me to tell you that, now that you're no longer with the defense. Or prudent."

"Would it be safe to assume that it won't involve investigating Doyle Thayer Junior's activities in the weapons trade?"

"Sorry."

"You mentioned compensation. If you'll answer that question I'll call us square."

"Why is it so important?"

"It so happens I'm a detective, Mr. Dorrance. It's the kind of work that if you're going to be any good at it at all you have to have a thirst for answers. You can't expect me to get all worked up and then walk away without some kind of release. There's a name for women who do that."

"I'm not a woman," he rapped.

This unexpected piece of bitterness fluttered on the air for a moment. Then his expression softened.

"Sorry. It has to do with growing up with the name Leslie. I'll answer your question. No, I'm leaving the weapons angle alone. There's ample evidence that Thayer was a wife-abuser, which is where the sympathy lies today. Sixty percent of the population of Detroit owns guns. I don't want to risk making him a hero: The Right to Bear Arms and all that."

"It's a big thing to ignore."

"The court is justice in a vacuum, Mr. Walker. Everything is simpler inside those marble walls; antiseptic. A great deal of trouble is taken to see that it remains so. This involves protecting jurors from those pesky little truths that can only confuse them. The average guy in the gallery who watches the news on television, incompetent though it is, knows more about the case being tried than the jury does. That's no accident."

"One other question. It won't involve confidences."

"Shoot." His eyes flicked toward the Luger on the end table and he laughed self-consciously.

"Do you expect to win this one?"

He laughed again, not self-consciously. "Nobody wins anything anymore outside of sports. Oh, your occasional state lottery player beats odds of ten million to one, but there's no skill involved and all he's really won is the opportunity to fend off mythical relatives to the end of his days, or at least of his fortune. Even our wars peter out with both sides claiming victory. The best a modern lawyer can hope for is

to make a legal point or two and get his name in the Giant
Golden Book of Precedents. If you're asking me if I expect
to do that, the answer is yes. In my crowd that's winning."

"For you. What's your client got to look forward to?"

"Appeals. It's all a system of raises and calls and raises
again, and the winner's the one who buys the pot." He studied me. "Are you shocked?"

"Vindicated is the word. I never thought it'd be a lawyer
that did it. Thanks for being candid."

"Thanks for not showing me the door." He stood and
stuck out his hand.

I got up and took it. "Who's going to play you in the TV
movie?"

"I rather like this fellow Chamberlain. He doesn't look
anything like me. Well, good-bye."

I went out with him and pulled my car out of the driveway so he could leave. In the street I sat watching the BMW
gliding down the block until a horn behind me pointed out
I wasn't alone on the planet.

Later, after I had put the car in the garage, I thawed out
a roast beef dinner and chased it with cold beer while watching the conclusion of a miniseries starring a former movie
queen who had outlived all her scandals to win a couple of
lifetime achievement awards. They hadn't improved her acting one bit. I only half-watched it in any case. The job was
over, it was time to think about the next one. I was past the
age when it was fun to stew over what was finished, or to
insert myself where I would be about as popular as the Cal-
cutta Burger King. There was no percentage in pursuing a
dead case; nothing to be gained except a contempt-of-court
citation and a long unpaid vacation after my license was
lifted. Only an idiot would consider it.

I went to bed before the end of the movie. I wanted to be
fresh when I asked Ma Chaney how much she knew about
Doyle Thayer Jr.

══7══

WE GOT SOME RAIN during the night, a ten-minute downpour that started and ended as suddenly as if a nozzle had been twisted. The pavement was still dark with moisture when I hit it after breakfast and the sky was overcast, making one of those days muffled in damp dirty cotton that make you sweat while standing motionless in the shade. It was as good a day as any to visit the country.

Emma Chaney lived in rural Macomb County, in a tired white clapboard house that probably wasn't much different from the one she had been born in on the Kentucky-Tennessee border sometime around the First World War. The daughter of a country gunsmith who fathered no sons, she was said to have learned to field-strip and reassemble a Browning automatic rifle blindfolded by the age of ten. If that was an exaggeration, she had certainly picked up everything there was to know about percussion weapons since that time. At thirteen she had married a big-knuckled farmer whose livelihood blew away with the Dust Bowl in

1933, after which he took a job on the Ford line at River Rouge and moved North with his wife and the first of four sons. When a defective propane tank blew up twenty years later, smearing Calvin Chaney over the morning's run of 1953 Fairlanes, Ma buried what they could scrape up of him, used the out-of-court settlement to pay off the house, and went into the gun trade to keep supper on the table.

Her sons, grown by this time, had opted for the more active end of the same business. Jesse, the oldest, had had his head blown off his shoulders by a riot gun while fleeing a botched bank robbery in Houston. Floyd was in Florida awaiting execution on three counts of felony murder. Wilbur had a room to himself in the criminal ward of the Forensic Psychiatry Center in Ypsilanti, and Mason, the baby, was in his third year on the FBI's Ten Most Wanted list for a series of armored car robberies in Kansas City; although it was common knowledge to everyone but the Feds that he visited his mother at home on a regular basis.

One thing the Feds did know, along with everyone else to whom such things mattered, was that if the job called for anything from popguns to primacord, Ma Chaney was the woman to see. She had eleven arrests and only one conviction, for failure to notify her insurance company that she was storing six cases of smokeless powder in an upstairs closet. She had been fined and released. Since then no search warrant had managed to turn up anything more volatile than a can of Campbell's pork and beans.

There were clumps of gravel on the burned-out lawn and tufts of dead grass in the driveway, or maybe it was the other way around. When I climbed out of the car, a tethered goat with its hipbones showing studied me with brown tilted eyes, then resumed gnawing the paint off a corner porch post. On the porch I pulled my shirt away from my back, put on my plaid summerweight sportcoat, and rapped on the screen door. A strong smell of frying onions drifted out.

"I know you. Ma never forgets a face."

The woman unhooked the screen door and pushed it open against the spring. She didn't stand a half-inch above five feet, but she was just as broad, wrapped in a canary yellow nylon kimono with neon orange pomegranates on it in bunches. Her hair had been hennaed to match the pomegranates and gone over with an antique curling iron, leaving girlish ringlets around the gross face, powdered an eighth of an inch deep and painted with rouge and eyeliner, as if a Mary Kay lady had gone berserk and she had been standing in her path. The eyes themselves were round and black, without shine, and a cigarette smoldered on her lower lip.

"Well, come ahead in," she barked. "You're invited, but the flies ain't."

I stepped inside then. As many times as I had laid eyes on Ma, the sight was always rough on the motor functions.

"Didn't expect you before lunch. Place is a mess." She let the screen door bang and shuffled past me in bunny slippers to lift last night's *News* off a sofa with doilies on the arms and birds of paradise needlepointed on the cushions. Something else, much smaller, went into the pocket of her kimono before I could get a look at it. The living room had been decorated straight out of the furniture commercials on the afternoon Charlie Chan movie, beginning with one of those revolving-shade forest fire table lamps and ending with glow-in-the-dark bullfighters on black velvet in phony gilt frames on the printed wallpaper. Knickknacks were everywhere, but except for the newspaper there wasn't a scrap of unplanned clutter or a streak of dust in sight. The place was a mess, all right.

Ma crammed the newspaper into a lacquer wastebasket with a peacock on it and took a seat in a big overstuffed rocker that left her feet dangling. "Sit yourself down, son. Only not so hard you can't get your wallet loose." She laughed and started coughing. The cigarette teetered.

"It'll be quick." I chose a maple upright, the only seat in the room that didn't look as if it would swallow me whole. "I need to know if you ever had business with a man named Thayer, or if anyone you know had business with him. I'm not looking to put anyone in Dutch. It's worth something to my client."

She stopped coughing. "How much?"

"That depends on what you can tell me."

"I won't tell you till you pay me and you won't pay me till I tell you. I sure hope you brought lunch."

That was it for a while. I sat, she rocked, an antique oscillating fan perched on a windowsill swooped back and forth. I began to look forward to the breeze on the back of my neck.

"Five hundred," I said. "If you can tell me something about Thayer I don't know, or point me in the direction of someone who can."

She rocked a little more. "What's to stop you from saying you knew it already after I tell it? If I got it to tell."

"If I didn't pay my freight you wouldn't be talking to me now."

"Folks change."

"Like hell they do."

She rocked. Then: "Well, I never dicker. Either it's the right price or it ain't, and Ma's too old to sit here in the heat trading horses."

I lit a cigarette and waited.

"Hubert!" she bellowed.

I said, "Who's Hubert?"

"One of the darlings."

I was turning that one over when the screen door banged and a big man with greasy blond hair came in chewing gum with his mouth open. He was wearing a brown polyester suit that bagged in the knees. He had a pale, pockmarked face, flat blue eyes, and a hearing aid in his right ear. I knew him, of course. I thought I even knew the suit.

"Yeah, Ma." He hesitated when he saw me, but showed no recognition, only an impersonal sort of suspicion that went with his Georgia drawl.

"Hubert Darling, this here's Amos Walker. Hubert's been useful around here with the boys away. He's going to see if you're wearing a wire. You won't mind."

I said, "How's he going to do that?"

She hopped off the rocker; for a woman of her age and figure she had plenty of spring. "It's time Ma went up and got dressed. This here northern living's making her lazy. You be thorough, now, Hubert. There's plenty other places to tape them on besides the chest." She shuffled out.

Hubert's blue eyes looked like painted tin. "Stand up and get 'em off," he said.

I stood. Face to face, I had an inch on him. The bigness was attitude, nothing more. "You don't remember me, do you?"

"Am I supposed to?"

"You held me once while your brother Jerry went over me with a set of brass knuckles. It was in a trailer park not far from here."

"Jerry's in Jackson. He don't get out till December."

"When did they let *you* out?"

"Get 'em off," he snarled. "The shoes and socks too."

"You still don't know me."

"Mister, if I had a nickel for every trailer park I been in and every time I held somebody for Jerry." His breath smelled of Juicyfruit. "You want me to take 'em off you?"

"Maybe this'll help." I hit him with one hundred and eighty-five pounds.

He was solid. He rocked back on his heels without going over. But he was too dazed to react right away, and I hit him again just as hard. He backpedaled and lost his balance. I reached past him and plucked the forest fire lamp off its table just before it tipped over. He was out then, but his body didn't know it. He rolled onto his stomach and tried to

push himself up. I hit him on the head with the lamp.
Bright yellow-and-orange bits of painted forest fire sprayed
all over. He groaned and fell on his face.

"Hubert?" Ma's wheezy voice barely reached the ground
floor.

I dropped what was left of the lamp, stepped over Hubert, and pulled the newspaper out of the lacquer wastebasket. I wondered what a day-old copy of the Detroit *News* was
doing lying around an otherwise tidy living room.

The answer was on the front page, or rather missing from
it. Someone with scissors had snipped an L-shaped piece out
of the lower right-hand corner. I thought I knew where it
had wound up.

"Hubert?" Footsteps shuffled on the stairs.

I put the paper back the way I'd found it. I didn't need
it as much as I needed Ma's goodwill. Around Detroit, old
newspapers are as easy to get hold of as hired muscle.

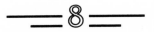

S HE CAME IN wearing boys' Size Husky overalls over a
man's plaid flannel shirt and sneakers on her big square
feet. With her orange hair and the paint and powder
on her face the outfit made her look like one of those in-
flatable clowns that pop back up when you punch them. She
looked down at Hubert Darling, then nudged the wreckage
of the lamp with a toe. "My Calvin gave me that."

"Sorry. His head was harder than it looked."

"He dead?"

"Only from the neck up," I said. "You won't notice the
difference."

"Well, if they had any brains Ma couldn't afford them."
She booted him in the ribs, hard enough to bruise one.
"Wake up, peckerhead."

"Let him snooze. He's going to come to with a headache a
yard wide."

"One thing's sure. Nobody that ever wore no wire ever hit
anybody that hard."

"You'd be surprised." I'd stopped at my bank on the way there. I took five fifty-dollar bills out of my wallet, righted the table that had been knocked over, and laid them on top. Their edges stirred a little in the wind from the fan. "You'll have to trust me for the other half. I've got a car payment due."

"What about your client?"

"That's a little complicated."

"Complicated how?"

"What about Thayer?" I asked.

She booted Hubert again. "Sure he ain't dead?"

"I could go out and get my gun and come back and put a bullet in him if you like. It'd be quicker than kicking him to death."

"It ain't that. I just don't need no bodies rolling around like out at the barn that time. I live here. Well." She set fire to a cigarette, striking a wooden kitchen match off a thick thumbnail the way I never could, and coughed, hacking a little and swallowing.

"January it was," she said. "Maybe February. One of them cold months when I get to thinking about visiting my boy Floyd in Florida. They bum-rapped him down there. He told me himself he was in Arkansas when them boys shot that feller in Fort Lauderdale. My boys steal, but they don't lie."

"January or February," I prompted.

"He had a letter with him. I got it here." She took a fold of coarse paper out of the slash pocket of her overalls and handed it to me.

The sheet had yellowed in a drawer, been doodled on, and used to add sums of figures in Ma's crabbed hand. The message had been badly typed on a machine whose *o*'s and *a*'s looked like fat periods.

>   Ma
>   Well how the hell are you i guess you remember
>   your old freind Sturdy. This heres junior hes OK

The moronic signature at the bottom might have read "Sturdy." It might have read John Hancock or Pontius Pilate. I said, "That'd be Waldo Stoudenmire, the Iroquois Heights fence?"

"Maybe."

I returned the letter. "I didn't know Sturdy dealt guns."

"Sturdy'd peddle his grandmother's teeth if there was cash in it." She refolded the letter and pocketed it. "But he knows what's good for him and he don't give nobody the green light here that didn't earn it."

"Describe Thayer."

She squinted up at me through the smoke of her cigarette. "Thirty. Your build, but soft around the middle. Be fat in a couple. Glasses, I think."

"Sounds like his pictures. What was he after?"

"You come back with that other two-fifty and Ma will tell. Plus thirty for the lamp. I forgot about the lamp."

"I could just ask Sturdy."

"Sturdy's dead, I heard."

"I didn't."

"You will."

I scratched my chin. "It's like that, is it?"

"Not Ma. Ma don't kill nobody. She just hears things. You young blades forget us old folks are around."

"Did you make a sale?"

"I ain't in business not to."

"For how much?"

"Ten."

"Thousand?"

She coughed. "No, Cadillacs. Of course ten thousand."

"Cash?"

"Check."

"Check?" For some reason that rocked me harder than the part about Sturdy being dead. "Since when do you put anything on the books?"

"The books say I sold him the truck I made the delivery with," she said. "Or would of."

"You didn't deliver?"

"Bank wouldn't cash the check."

"He stopped payment?"

"Not him. His old man. The bank told me."

"How could Doyle Thayer Senior stop payment on a check his son wrote?"

"He can when it's drawn on his account." She tidied the bills, folded them, and put them inside her bib pocket. "That there's worth about two-fifty, I'd say. Come back with the rest and I'll tell you the rest."

I sighed, took out my wallet, and gave her the other half of the five hundred. "I still owe you for the lamp."

She chortled; that's all you could call it. She counted the money and put it with the rest. "Don't never play poker with a lady from Logan County."

"What was Junior buying?"

"Well, if I was the kind to deal in guns and such, and if Junior was the kind to buy from me, I might offer him a *Po*laris missile."

"For ten thousand?"

"Just the shell. Ma don't mess around with that nuke juice."

"Where'd you get a Polaris missile?"

"I didn't. I just told you, I ain't the kind, and if I was, I wouldn't say so for no five hunnert."

I looked down at Hubert Darling, who had begun groaning again but showed no signs of moving. Sorting through my terminology. "Where would someone go around here to lay hold of a Polaris missile, shell or otherwise?"

"Talk to the Colonel."

"Colonel who?"

Her face was a mask; but then it was anyway. "If you don't know who the Colonel is, he don't want you to know. Ma's got to get lunch on the table." She pushed past me, in the direction of the smell of frying onions.

"If it's for Hubert, you better make soup out of it," I said. "He won't be chewing anything for a while."

"I forgot to ask why you hit him." She was in the kitchen now, banging pots and pans.

"Old times' sake." On my way out I crunched through pieces of broken lamp.

The onions had made me ravenous. I had lunch at a sausage palace a mile from the Chaney house. It was a block building made over to look like a barn, with a hip roof, red aluminum siding, and fat waitresses bound in tight pink uniforms. There was enough grease on my plate to lube a fleet of Chevies. I shoveled it in with both hands.

Afterwards I smoked and thought. I wondered who the Colonel might be and what army he belonged to. I wondered what a spoiled kid with too much money wanted with a nuclear weapon that didn't work. I wondered what the article was that Ma had clipped out of last night's newspaper and stuck in the pocket of her nutty kimono. I wondered, while digesting lunch, who was going to pay for supper.

My waitress, three hundred pounds with yellow hair in a bun and *Dora* stitched across her apron pocket, brought my bill. "Can I get you anything else?"

"Not unless there's a copy of yesterday's *News* in the kitchen," I said.

"I think it was in your soup." She laid the bill on the table, but she didn't go away. "You look like a man with problems."

"I'm out of work."

"Put your wife to work. That's what my husband did."

"I don't have a wife."

"I wish I didn't have a husband."

I covered the bill, emptying my wallet for the second time

in two days. "What would you call a man who gets fired, then goes on doing the same job without pay?"

"He working for a woman?"

"Yeah."

She counted her tip and put it in her apron. "I'd call him a romantic. But only if he tips twenty percent."

Back in the city I got some more cash and stopped at a corner bar for a cold beer and a slice of conditioned air. While the bartender was drawing the beer I used the pay telephone by the rest rooms to call my answering service. Waiting for the girl to come on the line I belched sausage.

"Yes, Mr. Walker, a Mr. Scooter called at ten o'clock. He wants you to call him back. You know the number, he said."

"Shooter," I corrected. "Anything else?"

"A woman called a few minutes ago, but she wouldn't leave her name."

"Maybe it was Dora."

"Pardon?"

"Nothing. I just needed some advice." I thanked her and hung up.

Shooter's line was busy. I called Detroit Police Headquarters and asked for Inspector Alderdyce.

"Alderdyce."

"Congratulations, John," I said. "I didn't get my invitation to your promotion party."

"I'll throw a party the day I leave this job. I inherited four murders and a series of home invasions from Grosse Pointe to Flatrock. How are you, Walker?"

"Working, sort of. I was wondering if some cold meat named Waldo Stoudenmire had happened across your desk yet."

He jumped on it. "Who says Sturdy's dead?"

"The word's on the street, like they say on TV. Where *is* the Street, anyway?"

"Hollywood. If you hear anything else, let me know.

Sturdy's the one I wanted to talk to about these home invasions. The scroats have to be laying the stuff off somewhere."

"I'll keep you in mind. You're my first friendly inspector."

"I'll say." He let the hard edge go. "Remember Proust?"

"I thought I could forget him when he left the department. Then he got indicted up in the Heights and I thought he was forgotten. He's still in office."

"He'll be retired before he sees court. In the Heights they take crime off the streets and put it in city hall where they can keep an eye on it."

I belched into a fist. "What do you know about a guy who calls himself the Colonel?"

"He's got a white beard and sells chicken by the bucket."

"I needed a funny inspector today," I said. "That's the only thing the day was missing."

"We're here to serve."

We said good-bye. I worked the cradle and dialed again.

"You're a hard man to reach," Shooter said.

"What've you got for me?"

"Eleven o'clock tonight, same place. Leave the heat behind. Man hates heat unless he's buying it or selling it."

"What's the man's name?"

He laughed and broke the connection.

Three people were waiting to use the telephone. I pegged the receiver and went back to the bar to drink my beer, which was just cool by this time. I drank it anyway. When you're broke you respect the little investments.

At my building I paused to poke through the trash basket on the corner. Any other day there would have been four or five old copies of the Detroit *News* in it; today it was the *Free Press* and sixteen not-quite-empty cartons from the Chinese take-out place in the next block. I gave up.

Upstairs in my reception room, Constance Thayer looked up from an old magazine and told me I had a piece of Mandarin orange on my lapel.

—=9=—

I PLUCKED THE PIECE of spoiled fruit off my jacket and dropped it in the smoking stand. The glamour of detective work never dims.

I unlocked the door to the inner office and held it for her. The suit was tan today, the blouse gold and caught at the neck with a jade brooch in an antique gold setting. She carried a brown leather handbag into the office and leaned it against one leg of the customer's chair when she sat down. With some women the things are just props. Her hair was red in the sunlight.

On my way in I picked up the mail under the slot, sat down behind the desk, and shuffled through it. There were no checks today, just bills and a letter with the stylized owl that Reliance Investigations used for a logo printed in the corner. I knew what it would contain, but since she didn't seem in a mood to talk just yet I opened it. It was computer-printed on stiff steel-gray stock to match the envelope and Krell's shrapnel tie clasp. This one should have been pink. I read it a second time more slowly, just as if I were alone, then laid it aside and folded my hands on the blotter like Barry Fitzgerald.

"Was yesterday morning a special occasion, or does a drink any old time of the day sound better than a kick in the teeth?" I asked.

"I — I'd like a drink very much."

I brought up the bottle and two glasses. I wasn't sure about them, so I took them into my little water closet, washed them, and splashed an inch of water into each, letting it run first. Back at the desk I colored the water and handed her one. I raised the other.

"Carthage must be destroyed."

She laughed slightly and we clinked glasses. Although she looked like a sipper, she took the top off hers like a steeplejack. An orange flush climbed her cheeks under the tan.

"Do you always keep it in the drawer?" she asked. "Like a gumshoe?"

"I did a job for a cabinetmaker once who offered to install one of those trick bars that come out from behind the paneling. But I'd have had to walk clear across the office."

"I didn't drink or use anything at all when I met Doyle, not even when I made those films. He got me started with Irish coffee. That was before the cocaine."

"Still do it?"

She shook her head. "I'm allergic to the smell of hundred-dollar bills."

"Me too."

She smiled politely. I had some more and set my glass on the blotter. "You talked to Dorrance?"

"Yes. He was very angry with Mr. Krell for hiring you without consulting him."

"Krell has some old-fashioned ideas. He thinks he can run his own business his own way."

"You sound as if you admire him. Yesterday I had the impression —"

"The right one. But he's his own man, even if it's on his wife's money, and he employs only the best. Those that will put up with him, anyhow; they generally don't for long." I folded my hands again. Body language. "You didn't come here to write a book about Ernest Krell."

"I came here to re-hire you."

"Does Dorrance know?"

"He thinks I'm home. I tried to call you earlier, but your service said you were out. I took a chance on catching you here."

"Where's home these days?"

"I'm staying with my sister in Redford." She studied me. "You think I'm a coward, don't you?"

"No woman who ever shot a man for beating her up is."

She dismissed that with a jerky impatient wave. Cocaine gestures are a long time going. "I have confidence in you, Mr. Walker. I realize my character judgment is suspect, considering the man I married, but I liked the way you refused to let Mr. Krell intimidate you yesterday. Leslie was impressed, too, based on his meeting with you last night. I think it would take a lot to make you give up an investigation."

"More than you'd think."

"I guess I really am a coward. If I weren't I'd fire Leslie because of my faith in you. But —"

"But the hearing is in less than three weeks and a retired Supreme Court justice couldn't do the necessary homework in that time to bring himself up to where Dorrance is now. You could get a continuance, but not in Iroquois Heights, and not in an election year, and not when the father of the man you killed is Doyle Thayer Senior. You don't owe anyone any explanations, Mrs. Thayer. Least of all me."

She picked up her purse, opened it, and laid a bank money order on the desk. It was made out to A. Walker Investigations in the amount of three thousand dollars. I'd been wrong about the purse being only a prop.

The ante was going up.

"Naturally," she said, "the court has frozen our joint assets, Doyle Junior's and mine. But as you can see, I have my own sources."

I didn't pick up the money order. I took the cap off the bottle and freshened our glasses. Said nothing.

She said, "For months I'd been selling off the jewelry Doyle gave me and putting the money in an account he didn't know about. I had paste copies made so he wouldn't miss the pieces. There's much more where that came from."

"Does Dorrance know that part?"

"He's my lawyer, not my confessor."

"Tell him."

"Why? It's not his business."

"Your business is everybody's business when you're on the hook for murder. In this case he'll need to know it for when the prosecution throws it at you as motive."

"Doyle *gave* me the jewelry. I had a right to sell it and I have a right to use the money as I see fit."

"That's how you see it. The other side will say you'd been deceiving Doyle for months and were afraid he'd catch on. Then they'll use his history of wife-beating against you. They might even say you'd been planning to kill him all that time, that you were preparing a getaway stake. Given the time lapse between your last workover and when you shot him, your self-defense plea is already too shaky to withstand that kind of reasoning."

"They won't know about it. Unless you tell them."

I scribbled four names on my telephone pad, tore off the sheet, and slid it across the desk. "Is one of these the jeweler you sold the stuff to?"

She looked at the sheet. Her expression said it all.

"What you've been doing isn't new," I said. "Those four specialize in buying jewelry from housewives in Grosse Pointe, Bloomfield Hills, and the Heights, making good cop-

g the originals outside the state. That last
t. Their sources can't afford to have the dia-
Hubby gave them last Christmas show up in
res on Valentine's Day." I pointed at the money
.at's your maiden name?"
.sitated, then nodded.

"I. .ecil Fish, who is the Iroquois Heights prosecutor,
hasn't run your married and maiden names and every possible combination past every bank in the area in search of a
secret account, he's a lot more stupid than he was the last
time I saw him. By now he knows about the money, has put
two and two together, which is what two and two are for,
and is already working on those four names. Crooked politicians aren't always dumb. Not even usually."

The speech had had its effect. Her fingers shook a little
when she took the pack of Pall Malls out of her handbag
and put one to her lips.

"That's the trouble with being basically honest." I lit it for
her. "When you do get tricky you haven't had any practice."

She blew smoke deliberately at the money order. "Do you
think it was a getaway stake?"

"It doesn't make any difference what I think. People are
always asking anyway."

"Well, that's just what it was. I was getting set to run. I
had no chance of taking our son with me if we divorced;
Doyle's father would've seen to that. Without me around to
hit, it would be just a matter of time before Doyle got
zonked enough to hurt Jack. The money was for us to get
away and to live on until I found a job somewhere else, under another name."

"What kind of a job?"

It must have come out differently from the way I'd intended. Anyway her hazel eyes got hard.

"I'd make films again if I had to. You do what you can to
survive. When it's you and your son you do more."

"Why didn't you run?"

"I should have. I didn't." She used my ashtray. "I told myself I wasn't ready, that I needed more money to be truly secure. That's the kind of trap you get into when you go to live in a big house where someone else pays the bills. I'd probably still be there, playing the good wife during the week and selling pearls on Saturday, if that one night he hadn't beat me so hard I'm still passing blood.

"No, I'm not a coward, Mr. Walker. No more than most. I'm not courageous either. Or I wasn't, until that night."

I looked at the money order. I still hadn't touched it. "Did you see anyone following you here?"

"No one followed me."

"Sure they did. You've had a tail on you since you made bail. That's how it works. Well, if the law has access to your bank records they know about this money order and who it's for, so it doesn't much matter. Tell Dorrance about the account. And tell him I'm back on the case."

"*Are* you back on the case?"

I picked up the money order and put it in the top drawer of the desk. "It's more than I ask for in a retainer, but the expenses are running high on this one. If there's anything left when the thing is done, you'll get it back, minus my day rate."

"Can you start right away?"

"I never stopped."

The look I'd seen before came into her eyes then. I cut her off.

"Don't put on the cap and veil just yet, Mrs. Thayer. It so happened I had nothing to do this morning and no bills to pay. I'm not in the hero business."

"I didn't mean to imply that you were." She put a hand on one of mine. It was cool and dry as before. "Thank you."

"Where can I reach you?"

She picked up the pencil I'd used before and wrote a Redford address and telephone number on my pad. Then she rose. "I hope Leslie doesn't quit when I tell him."

"He wouldn't quit this one if you confessed to first-degree murder on *Donahue*." I got up to let her out.

When the outer door closed behind her, I went back to the desk and finished my drink. Then I poured myself another without water and read the money order. It had a lot of zeroes, just like the case so far. After a while I put it in my wallet and left for my bank, where the girl behind the counter smiled at me for the first time in two days.

From there it was only a block to the party store where Marcus worked. In the storeroom I mopped the back of my neck with a handkerchief and watched him stacking crates of bottles until he had time to pull a copy of last night's *News* out of a pile. I gave him two bucks.

"You know, Mr. Walker, you can get that free if you ask up front." Today he had on a yellow T-shirt, dark with sweat, with a Monster truck rampant on his chest.

"Yeah, but then I wouldn't get to come back here and read your clothes."

"You after a killer?"

"Actually, I'm working for one."

Outside the store I unfolded the paper and looked at the lower right-hand corner. The item that Ma Chaney had clipped out of her copy and stuck in a pocket ran a column and a half, with a double heading:

FIFTH AREA HOME INVADED
Intruders Threaten Couple with Automatic Weapons

=10=

THE SIDEWALK WAS NO PLACE to give the article any
concentration, but I wasn't ready to go back to the office. I folded the paper and carried it to the little lot
where I parked my car. Sitting there sweating in the sun
with all four windows open, I read it.

> Police have linked the armed invasion of a house
> in the 1600 block of Pembroke last night with four
> previous robberies conducted in the Detroit met-
> ropolitan area over the past two weeks.
>   Shortly after 8:00 P.M. yesterday, police said,
> four men in ski masks and armed with light auto-
> matic rifles burst through the front door of a
> house occupied by Dr. Anton Juracik and his wife
> Marian and threatened to kill the couple if they
> did not surrender all the cash and drugs in the
> house. When Dr. Juracik resisted, one of the in-
> truders struck him in the face with the butt of his
> weapon, knocking him unconscious, police said.

According to police, Mrs. Juracik then turned over an undisclosed amount of cash, whereupon she was struck on the side of the head with a blunt instrument which police believe to have been either the barrel or the butt of an automatic rifle. Police said the bandits then ransacked the house and left with a videocassette recorder, two color television sets, a number of stereo components, and jewelry valued at $18,500.

Dr. Juracik was treated for a broken nose at Detroit General Hospital and released later in the evening. Mrs. Juracik remains in critical condition there with a fractured skull and a severe concussion.

"This robbery is definitely connected with similar actions which occurred in Detroit, Grosse Point, Iroquois Heights, and Flatrock within the last two weeks," reported Inspector John Alderdyce of the Detroit Police Department, who has been placed in charge of the investigation. "The police of all four communities are cooperating in this effort and we have a number of definite leads."

The article, which continued inside the first section, recapped the four previous robberies, including a casualty count of six injured homeowners and an estimated take totaling $110,000.

Alderdyce's statement was half lie and half sin of omission. The police of four neighboring communities couldn't cooperate in the same life raft, and the "definite leads" would number around ten thousand. I read the article again, then put the paper back together and tossed it into the back seat.

Despite her taste in clothes, make-up, furniture, and personnel, Ma Chaney was fastidious. She wouldn't save an article just because it caught her eye, but she'd be the type to keep a record. The targets of the five home invasions, all located in high-income neighborhoods and belonging to professional people approaching middle age, hadn't been chosen at random. The careful planning extended to the choice of weapons, full automatic rifles instead of the usual run of cheap revolvers and pump shotguns. You don't buy military assault weapons behind a diner on Sherman. For that you go to Macomb County.

I was weighing the pluses and minuses of going back there myself when the door on the passenger's side opened and a man climbed in beside me. He was slender, in an unlined powder-blue jacket and white duck pants that made him look cool despite the heat, and a cocoa straw hat with a narrow brim turned down in front. He had a thin, *café au lait* face with a mealy complexion and one of those pencil moustaches that would have looked more at home, like the man himself, with an all-white drill suit and a pitcher of margaritas on a verandah overlooking a firing squad.

"Amos Walker, I think." He had a slight, almost too slight, Latin accent. It had been worked on, then allowed to slip back, possibly in a fit of ethnic pride.

"Is that a question?"

"I'm Lieutenant Philip Romero. My chief would like to speak with you."

"Which chief would that be?"

He unbuttoned his jacket, exposing a bone-handled .38 in a holster with a gold shield pinned to it bearing the elaborate old-fashioned Iroquois Heights city seal.

"Oh," I said. "That chief."

11

LIEUTENANT ROMERO indicated a man in uniform standing next to the car on the driver's side. "That's Officer Pollard. He'll drive our car back while I ride with you. Unless you'd rather leave yours here."

Somehow I knew before I looked that Pollard would have a crew cut and Ray-Bans. "We met yesterday," I said. "What's the charge?"

"No charge. This isn't an arrest. It would just be a lot more convenient all around if you'd come with us."

"If that's a threat you did it nicely."

"When I make a threat, people don't ask me if I made one." He was waiting for an answer.

"I'll drive."

He shrugged; eloquently, of course. Where he came from shrugging is an art form.

Pollard got into an unmarked Pontiac parked in the next aisle and I started the Chevy. Romero wound up the window on his side.

"No air conditioning, sorry," I said.

"Don't need it. Take I-75."

We tooled along Grand River with the Pontiac behind. "Puerto Rico, right?"

"We're all Puerto Ricans to you Anglos. I came with the boatlift."

"It's a long way from Mariel to a gold shield in Iroquois Heights."

"We aren't all convicts. Some of us are baseball players."

"I thought you looked like a shortstop."

"Catcher. I was scouted for the Tigers." There was pride in his voice. "Ah, but you can't feed your children on a boy's dreams."

"Lousy batting average, huh."

"Worst in Toledo."

We didn't say much once we entered the expressway. It was Friday afternoon and all the lanes were clogged with RV's and boats on trailers pointed north. I lost sight of the Pontiac.

"Take the next exit," Romero said.

"That's the wrong way for downtown."

"I know it."

With him directing we followed a narrow paved road west of Iroquois Heights past a couple of shopping centers and then some houses. After a while the houses thinned out and we ran out of pavement. From there on, our way led between deep woods on both sides, with here and there a farm hacked out of the foliage. Crawling waves of heat flooded the hills ahead with imaginary pools of water. The Pontiac was visible now in the dust clouds behind us.

"Turn in here."

We had been traveling for three quarters of an hour. I swung around a dusty unmarked mailbox and followed two ruts through a stand of virgin pines with trunks nearly as big around as the car, over a hill, and into a clearing where a long white house with bottle-green shutters stood on ten acres of fresh sod. A large red barn loomed behind it and horses grazed inside whitewashed fences between the buildings.

We stopped in front of the house. Pollard braked behind us and our combined dust drifted forward and disappeared into the grass. As we were getting out, a rider who had been cantering a big chestnut around one of the corrals leaned down, unlatched the gate, and trotted up to the Chevy. It was Mark Proust, the Iroquois Heights deputy chief of police.

"Any trouble?" he asked Romero.

"No."

"I'll see you inside."

Gathering the reins, Proust looked down at me for the first time. He looked much older than he had the last time we'd met, his white hair thinner, his face grayer and more pouchy; but then I was used to seeing him in a business suit. He appeared thicker but strangely fit in an open-necked shirt, whipcord breeches, and knee-length boots. He turned the horse and cantered back toward the corral without a word in my direction. Lieutenant Romero and I watched.

"How long you figure he sat in that saddle waiting for us?" I asked.

"Horas." The lieutenant made a hoarse noise in his throat. "Hours."

Inside, a Hispanic maid in a white starched blouse and an orange skirt led us into a sun-drenched living room full of rustic furniture, exchanged pleasantries with Romero in Spanish, and left us.

"When did he get the ranch bug?" I asked.

"About the time his first granddaughter graduated high school."

Pollard said nothing. His uniform creaked when he shifted his weight. I looked at a recent painting over the fireplace of Proust in his riding clothes.

"Do you suppose he and Ernest Krell know each other?"

"*Qué?*"

I turned around. "We're awfully Old Country suddenly. I didn't hear any of that in the car."

"Sorry. Places like this bring out the *peón* in me."

"You were never a *peón*."

He shrugged again. "My father rolled cigars in a window in Havana."

"If I ever meet a Cuban whose father didn't roll cigars in a window, I'll buy him one."

He smiled briefly. He had very white teeth that transformed his face.

I had time to smoke a cigarette before Proust strode in from the back, pulling off his riding gloves. He smelled of sweat and leather.

"Our other guest is late," he told Romero. "Have you eaten today? Pollard?" The pair nodded.

I said, "I could go for a sandwich."

Proust turned his watery eyes on me. "Still the fucking smartass, aren't you?"

"I guess that means no sandwich."

"What's your business with the Thayer woman?"

"Never heard of her."

"Romero and Pollard followed her to your office."

"I lied."

He opened a cabinet with antlers for handles, sprayed seltzer into a glass, and filled it with bourbon. He was still holding his gloves in one hand.

"When they called in to report I told them to bring you here." He drank deeply. "Somebody wants to meet you."

"Why didn't Thayer send for me himself?"

He slammed down the glass, splashing whiskey, and swung on Romero. "Which one of you told him?"

"We didn't."

The simple dignity of the statement made Proust back up. "How'd you guess?" he asked me.

"Detective lessons cost money."

He fingered the gloves. He wanted to slap me with them. He swallowed the urge, along with the rest of the bourbon.

"Doyle Thayer isn't in the habit of leaving his office during working hours to talk to cheap private detectives. What made you think it's him?"

"You get these little beads on your upper lip when the subject is money," I said. "Thayer's got all of it in the Heights that the politicians haven't sniffed out. Speaking of working hours, how come *you're* not at the office?"

"I'm on vacation."

"Under suspension, you mean. When's your preliminary?"

"September first. The whole thing's a joke."

"Eleven counts is hilarious, all right," I said. "Long date. Figures. Constance Thayer's comes up in three weeks. But she's only up for murder."

"So you *are* working for her." You could smell the canary on his breath. Also bourbon.

"I'm working for her, yeah. That's what you wanted to find out. Can I go?"

"What are you doing for her?"

I looked at Romero. "You were wrong. He didn't want to talk to me."

"I'm wrong a lot," he said.

I jerked a thumb at Pollard. "What about him? I know he speaks because I heard him yesterday."

Pollard creaked his uniform. "You may hear me once too often, creep."

"Leave us alone, will you?" Proust said. Romero hesitated. "I'm not going to shoot him, for chrissake."

The pair left.

Proust stood slapping the gloves against his leg for a moment. Then he flipped them on top of the cabinet. "Have a seat."

I sat in a wingback chair with cowhide upholstery. It was as stiff as a trampoline.

"Drink?"

"I never drink before six."

"Bullshit." He refilled his glass. The seltzer bottle stayed put. "Let's not beat around the bush. We hate each other's guts and always have."

"Who's beating around the bush?"

"What we got here is a tramp who tanked up on booze and drugs and filled her husband full of lead. Not unusual these days, except the husband's father happens to be Doyle Thayer Senior, who employs half the population of the city I work for and pays taxes for the other half. Makes the police look bad; couldn't even protect one of its wealthiest citizens."

"The police *are* bad."

He let it pass. "On top of that, we got federal men poking around the house where the murder took place and they won't even tell us why. Doesn't matter that we know. And that's another thing: Where are the local authorities when a private individual is busy amassing the largest arsenal west of Fort Dix in his basement?"

"Riding horses?"

"Taking a piss, busting drunks for throwing up on a cop's shoes, it don't matter." His grammar was failing, a stormy sign. "There's an election in November and the spirit of reform is in the air. The sanctimonious little twerps smell blood. As if things would be any different six months after they took office."

"Another set of dirty underwear is still a change," I said.

That got to him. "You need our goodwill, you cheap son of a bitch. Who wants to hire a private eye who keeps getting doors slammed in his face?"

"I think I will have that drink."

He didn't move. I got up and went over and poured myself one, using the fizz. "My face is on every door between here and Port Huron," I said. "I'd rather be thrown down the back steps at Detroit Police Headquarters than invited into the Iroquois Heights city hall. This is good whiskey."

"I'd like to throw you down a few steps myself."

"Nice shack. Is it paid for?"

"It was a gift. From the grateful citizens of Iroquois Heights."

"In other words, Doyle Thayer."

"He's a citizen."

"Congratulations. Cecil Fish only got a boat, I heard. What about your boss the chief, or does he rate? He's been sick a long time."

"We're all friends here," he said. "Sure, I'm bought. Show me someone in public office who isn't, if not for money then for the promise of power. A lot of important work gets done anyway. Just because I'm not your idea of a servant of the people don't mean I don't do my job. Nobody's paying *me* to spring a murderer."

"Somebody's paying you plenty to see it doesn't happen."

"Where's the harm, if justice is served?"

"You political cops are always talking about justice when you mean the law," I said. "Every election you run ads promising equal justice, as if there were any other kind. You can't serve justice, and you sure as hell can't sell it. Whenever you try it turns into something else. Either it's there or it isn't. Iroquois Heights is where it isn't."

He straightened to his full height. It pushed out his paunch a little. He needed the horse. "You ought to be more grateful. I had you in jail once. Inmates have been known to hang themselves in their cells."

"I'm supposed to thank you because I didn't?"

"It could still happen."

"Romero told me I wasn't under arrest. Okay, what's the beef so I can order the rope?"

"I didn't mean now. Right now you're under safe conduct because it's in my best interest to keep you that way. I meant later. These charges they got against me are so much chickenshit."

"If I were you I'd worry about hanging my*self*. Some of the people who've been paying you for all this good police work you've been doing might not want you to turn state's evidence against them."

That hadn't occurred to him. He scowled down at his glass, but he didn't like the fortune he read there. He emptied it and set it down.

"What were you doing at Thayer Junior's place yesterday?" he said.

"Trying to keep from being blown clear to Lansing, mostly. You ought to get in on the auction. The department could use another fifty-caliber machine gun, I bet. For interrogations."

"Jesus Christ. Don't you ever quit?"

"Not unless the job quits me first."

"I'll see they put that on your headstone." The doorbell rang. "That's Thayer Senior. Ever met him?"

"Never."

"He's a corker."

The maid came in and announced the corker.

═ 12 ═

H E CAME IN SLOWLY, but without hesitating; he
hadn't entered anyplace uncertain of his welcome in
more than fifty years. Although he was not especially
tall, his trim build and a way he had of carrying his back
created an impression of considerable height. He appeared
at first to be totally bald, but at closer range his hair was pale
and cropped very short on a skull like a Roman emperor's,
the brow high and round. His nose was hooked, his eyes
dark and set deep. His suit wasn't important; it would be a
color and fabric that was right for him and he would know
where to go to have it cut and fitted. As he walked he
dragged his right foot very slightly. I'd read somewhere that
he had suffered a stroke a year or so back. He made it seem
like a temporary annoyance.

"Right on time, Mr. Thayer," said Proust, shaking the old
man's hand.

"I'm late. Two of your men are outside. I understood this
would be a private meeting." His voice was shallow. It often
is with men who seldom have to raise it.

"It will be. I asked Lieutenant Romero and Officer Pollard to escort Walker here. I can send them back anytime."

"Are you asking me if you may?"

"I'll send them back." It sounded lame to him too. Quickly he introduced us.

Thayer let me come to him; the less he walked the less he broadcast the limp. His grip was as frail as a dowager's. Up close, his head shook as from palsy, although the muscles on the sides of his jaw stuck out from the effort to control it.

"Is there someplace less open?" he asked Proust.

"The den is this way."

A short sunlit corridor lined with framed photographs of thoroughbreds led to a walnut door, which Proust unlocked and opened, standing aside to let us enter. It was a small woodstained room with an olive-colored rug, a big square desk with a mirror finish and nothing on top, and brass-plated trophies on the bookshelves. No books. A single window looked out on the corrals. Proust stepped past us and drew the curtains.

"I'd like this private," Thayer said. "Just Mr. Walker and me."

Proust's hesitation made his eyebrows rise.

"He's afraid I'll hit you with the desk, leap out the window onto a horse, and gallop away," I said.

The old man's face was without humor. "Were you brought here under force?"

"It was polite enough."

Proust said, "You don't know Walker like I do, Mr. Thayer. Sometimes —"

"Please wait for us."

Proust took himself out. He almost bowed.

Thayer wandered behind the desk, a natural migration for him. He was outlined against the curtained window now. His complexion was paler than his hair, almost translucent blue, but it wouldn't be because of his blood. The son of an upholsterer, he had worked his way up from the machine room to the front office of a tool company that no longer made tools, then bought it to serve as the flagship for an industry whose main product was numbers on the New York Stock Exchange. Since then he had been acquiring local ball clubs, a fast food chain in California, and a Spanish castle, which he had ordered dismantled and shipped across the Atlantic to a Brooklyn dock where it sat in numbered crates awaiting removal to Mackinac Island and his twelve-acre estate. He had done all this almost with nobody's notice, and it would probably still be that way had not his son's violent death catapulted him into the public eye like a very rich cinder.

In another year, possibly two, he would begin the long slide, sinking in on himself like a grand old building grown too heavy for its foundation, but that summer he stood astride the loose collection of feudal fiefdoms that is the Detroit area business community, and looked it.

"I've employed the services of Reliance on a number of occasions," he said. "I assume that's why Krell went outside the agency in this case."

I said nothing. It was one reason I hadn't thought of.

"My son and I had nothing in common except our name," he went on. "My fault. You can't build a successful business and tend to family at the same time. One or the other must suffer, and no one who chose family ever had his picture on the cover of *Forbes*. After my wife's third attempt at suicide I placed her in a private hospital and sent Doyle Junior away to school. When he was expelled from that one I sent him to another. When he was arrested for car theft I arranged for his release and had the incident erased from the record. I suppose now I should have let him face the consequences of his actions, but you can always afford to be objective when it doesn't matter anymore.

"Doyle never showed an interest in anything his first twenty-one years, except embarrassing his father. When at last he developed an affection for firearms, I offered him a position in an arms factory in which I own a part interest in Colorado; but he didn't want that, or anything else from me except money. Which I gave him. Guilt perhaps. The fact is that aside from the job offer, the only time I ever actively took steps to change the course he chose for himself was when I tried to stop him from marrying the woman who eventually killed him."

His head shook. Clamping his fingers on the edge of the desk, he stopped it. He breathed in and out deeply. "I offered her money, of course. She turned it down. Of course. There was so much more to be made later."

"Did you threaten to disinherit your son?" My voice sounded funny in the room.

"I don't make threats I don't intend to carry out, although it was certainly implied. She saw right through that. Women of her sort are impossible to bluff. I will not have what I've built broken up to feed an already bloated government, and there is no love lost between myself and the people I employ now to help me run it. She sensed that. Whatever hash Doyle might make of it, I was determined that Thayer Industries would remain in the Thayer family. I still am," he added.

"Your grandson."

"My grandson. I haven't many years left, but I mean to make my stamp on the boy, as I never could with his father. As I said, I've always found time for business. It's taken me this long, and the tragedy of my son, to realize that in this case family *is* business. His mother won't have him. Not while there is blood in these veins."

"Even if it means framing her for murder?"

His chin came up another centimeter. "Where is the frame? She admits she killed him."

"She confessed to it," I said. "Whether or not it was murder is why the case is going to court."

"Michigan law is clear on just what constitutes self-defense."

"I'm glad it is for you, Mr. Thayer. It never has been for me or the local legal community, on anything. That's why the shelves in this room would be groaning with law books, if Deputy Chief Proust read books."

"Be that as it may. Please understand that vengeance is not my motive; Doyle was dead to me a long time before he stopped breathing. I simply do not wish to see my legacy squandered on strangers. I want custody of my grandson."

"That's not up to me."

"It is if you succeed in having her acquitted. That's why you're working for Reliance."

"I'm not working for Reliance."

For the first time he faltered. "My information —"

"Is correct up to last night," I finished. "Mrs. Thayer's attorney fired me. I got the official notice from Ernest Krell today."

"Are you saying this meeting is a waste of time?"

"In my business, no experience is wasted unless you wake up with a bump on your head, or don't wake up at all. I can't speak for your business."

"Why didn't Proust say something?" His head began to shake again.

"I gave up trying to think like people like Proust a long time ago."

"He's begun to take my support for granted." He folded his hands behind his back, filing Proust in a new drawer. "I'm very sorry to have taken up so much of your day. You're free to go, of course. Not that you ever weren't."

I stayed put. "As long as we're both here, I wonder if you might help me clear up a couple of things I'm curious about."

"I?"

"A woman named Chaney told me you'd stopped payment on a check your son gave her for ten thousand dollars. It had to do with the purchase of a Polaris missile, although it went down on the books as a flatbed truck. I can guess why you stopped payment, but I'd like to know how he came to draw a check on your account."

"Why would you want to know that now?"

"You like to watch the numbers going up on the big board; I imagine it has something to do with your success. I like answers. When a question goes unanswered my brain goes to bed hungry. I'm pretty good at what I do myself and I guess that's the reason, or one of them."

"Perhaps you've earned it," he said. "In any case, there is no harm in telling you now. Doyle Junior was forging checks in my name. The allowance I gave him wasn't enough, it seems, to feed his ridiculous hobby. As long as he didn't involve me or the business, I didn't care what he spent it on, but I won't have my own son playing me for a fool. A bank employee became suspicious and called to ask if I'd authorized the check. I stopped payment immediately, as I would have with the others had I known about them."

"Others?"

"There were four in all, made out to cash. The first three weren't questioned and showed up on my monthly statement. They were for considerably less than ten thousand. The statement arrived about the time I learned of the last check. My son was killed before I could confront him."

"There was no mention of it in the press."

"Certainly not. I just said I won't be made the public fool. Anyway, it had nothing to do with what happened." He had a sudden inspiration. "Unless you're accusing me of conspiring to murder my own issue over money."

I shrugged, not as well as Lieutenant Romero did. "You paid the bank employee to keep his mouth shut?"

"He is now assistant comptroller in my Iroquois Heights plant."

"Nice." I rolled a cigarette around in my fingers. Well, it had to be asked. "Was there a job for me if I quit the Thayer case?"

"Head of plant security. But only if I approved of what I saw during this meeting. My new assistant comptroller proved his worth by spotting the forgery. If I were to start offering employment to everyone who did me a favor, I'd be in receivership by Christmas. You'd have earned your salary, I promise you."

"I figured you'd be the carrot. I already got the stick from Proust."

"You said you were curious about a couple of things," he said. "What's the other?"

"Just a wild shot. Have you ever heard of a local character who calls himself the Colonel?"

"I know several colonels. Thayer Industries provides fuel solenoids for the army. You'll have to be more specific."

"This one deals in arms. I doubt he's connected with the military, but you never know. I thought maybe your son might have mentioned him."

"We never discussed his hobby except that one time. A good deal of bile came up during that conversation, but no colonels."

"Thanks for your help, Mr. Thayer."

"You mean, for satisfying your idle curiosity." The dark eyes glittered.

I paused. I'd made a mistake others probably had, to their regret: seen a sick old man where Doyle Thayer was standing.

"Yeah," I said.

After a long time he shook my hand. The palsy was under control now. Maybe it had been an act from the beginning. "Please ask Mr. Proust to come back in."

I did that and left the house before the two could compare notes.

Lieutenant Romero was leaning back against the Pontiac, smoking a long slim cigar in the shade of a big maple. Pollard sat behind the wheel. It was hot even there, but the Cuban hadn't sweated a drop. I asked him for a match. He tossed me a gunmetal lighter.

I used it and tossed it back. "What's a guy like you doing working for someone like Proust?"

"You don't know what kind of a guy I am."

"Call it a hunch."

"I was a policeman in Havana, before I got into trouble with the government. It's work I know. You don't step off the boat and join the New York Police Department, or even the one in Miami. Nor Detroit. But I like the weather here, I mean in the winter. Where I come from it's always like this."

"How do you stay straight?"

"By being a very good policeman. And by knowing when to look out the window."

"How do you stand it?"

"I think about my wife and daughters in Cuba."

"I see."

"Do you have children?"

"No."

"Then you don't see."

I finished the cigarette in silence and snapped away the butt. "Thanks for the light."

"*De nada*," he said. "That means —"

"I know what it means."

He shrugged.

— 13 —

I DIDN'T GO BACK to the office or call my answering service. I knew there would be a message from Proust or
Thayer. I bought a fresh copy of the *News* and pulled it
apart over coffee and a sandwich at a counter, but there was
nothing new on the home invasions and no mention of
Sturdy Stoudenmire, or of any stray corpses that might have
been his. I left the paper there and went home, where I unplugged the telephone. It looked like it had been ringing.

My appointment with Shooter was for eleven. I undressed,
set the alarm for nine-thirty, and stretched out on top of the
sheets, but I didn't sleep for a while. It was a humid evening
and the fan was just pushing the same sweaty air around, but
that wasn't why.

Lying to an old man who had just lost his son wasn't restful.
Letting him think what you wanted him to think in order to
get information without even bothering to lie wasn't any better. Even when it was an old man whose son and now whose
grandson represented nothing more to him than the survival
of the family trade. Sometimes in the work you took short-

cuts, then spent the time you saved wondering if you shouldn't have gone the long way to begin with. Then wondering about it you went to sleep and dreamed you had, and everything was fine and everyone was happy until you woke up. When you woke up that way enough times you found yourself old and alone and asking yourself why you bothered to wake up at all. Or maybe you didn't feel any different from all the other times; and that was worse, because as far as anything that counted was concerned, you were dead.

Fortunately, I woke up feeling rotten.

The temperature had gone down with the sun. A light ground fog rolled along the shiny pavement and lay in pools in the hollows. The Chevy dipped into them between hills, where moisture condensed on the windows and my own headlamps shone back at me, showing a tired jaundiced face in the windshield. The jaundice was from the yellow in the lamps.

I reached the warehouse district early as planned. I cut the lights and engine, coasted to a stop, and sat listening to the engine crackling as it cooled and the river slapping against the seawall on the other side of the railroad tracks. Then I reached up and loosened the bulb in the domelight so it wouldn't go on when I opened the door.

Outside the car, the night air touched the back of my neck like a scythe. The sky was still overcast, blocking out the moon and stars, but the river had a phosphorescence all its own, made of reflected electric light and luminous microscopic organisms and chemical pollutants, casting a blue-green glow over the squat ugly buildings and heaped rubble. Every few seconds a car would pass along Jefferson Avenue with a swish and a click. It was Friday night, and except for this one little dead spot the city writhed.

Using a stack of old pallets for a staircase, I climbed onto a worm-eaten dock and retreated into the shadows until my back touched clammy brick. From there I had a clear view of my car, or at least of those parts that shone in the phantom glow from the river. The butt of the Smith & Wesson .38, the one registered gun in my two-piece arsenal, made a solid knot against my right kidney; if there was one thing you learned in the work, it was to deck yourself in iron whenever they told you to come in unarmed. There, untouched by the lamps of the cars passing a block away, their beams smoky in the fog, I waited. The air lay like metal against my skin.

Somewhere on the Canadian side of the river, a tower clock struck eleven, the gongs carrying in the damp air with a resigned loneliness, like a single plane hanging in an empty sky. The last stroke had trailed off when Shooter's rattletrap pickup rolled with its lights off between two warehouses at a blind angle to where my car was parked and stopped with a creak of brakes. I stayed where I was. I was close enough to smell the heated metal of his radiator.

When after two minutes nothing happened, I started to come out of the shadows. Then I stopped. Behind the pickup, also with its lights off, a late-model sedan coasted between the warehouses and crunched to a halt with its front bumper almost touching the vehicle ahead. All its doors opened — no domelight came on — and four men came out in dark clothes with knitted watchcaps on their heads, cradling something in their arms. Their faces reflected no light and when they passed me, twenty feet away and four feet down, I saw that their faces were artificially blackened. I also caught a sharp whiff of gun oil.

Sprinting silently on rubber soles, they fanned out, two on each side of the Chevy, stopped, raised their weapons, paused, and began firing all at once. The guns rattled, spouting smoke and fire and brass cartridges that twinkled as they arced and fell, while bullets raked the car from one end to the other and back again, but concentrating on the front seat. Glass burst, metal clanged, a tire blew with a report louder than the weapons and the car sagged toward one corner. Steam whooshed out of the radiator and drifted in a great cloud toward Jefferson.

Then, as suddenly as it began, the firing stopped. A piece of glass fell with a tiny clank. By then the four were running back toward the sedan. Most of the doors were still open when the lights and engine came on with a roar and the car swung backward in a tight half-circle and then took off the way it had come, its tires spraying gravel.

I was moving too. I had drawn the Smith & Wesson without realizing it, and now I leaped from the loading dock onto a pile of discarded rails, caught my balance, clambered over it, and stepped onto another platform, this one made of crumbling concrete. Now I was directly over Shooter's pickup. As it started forward I lowered myself into the bed of the truck.

If Shooter felt the extra weight on the springs, he didn't show it. He turned on the headlamps, aimed the hood into the path where the rails had been pulled up, and accelerated with a lurch that almost took me off my feet, toward one of the side streets that led to Jefferson. Sirens hiccoughed in the distance.

The pickup's engine was as much of a surprise as its sound system. We must have been doing eighty when he hit the avenue and turned east, knocking a piece off the curb and throwing me into a sitting position, this time with my back against the tailgate. I held on to the gun and crawled forward along the bed, where he couldn't see me in the rearview mirror. The truck peeled rubber and swayed on its springs on the curves, but the tires never left the road. It was a bucket of rust on a brand-new frame with a mill that was built in heaven, or Indianapolis at the very least.

He didn't slow down until we had left the river far behind and were in the neighborhoods, the sirens falling off behind us. Then we glided down into a legal speed and observed stop signs and lights. I waited until we stopped at one, then threw a leg over the side of the box and reached down and grasped the handle on the passenger's door. It was unlocked.

14

ELLO, SHOOTER."
His reaction when I tore open the door and swung
into the seat beside him holding the revolver was
classic. He looked at me, his eyes and mouth fell open, and
he tried to do a number of things: claw for the Beretta on
the dashboard, punch the accelerator, bail out through the
door on his side. I swept the Smith & Wesson's barrel
against his forehead, twisted the pistol out of his grip — its
weight said he'd loaded it this time — hurled it over my
shoulder through the open door, and grabbed the wheel.
We were rocketing across a quiet intersection toward a light-
pole on the corner. I threw us into a sliding stop and hit
him again. He groaned and sagged against me. I pushed
him back and held him.

"I'd give you another lick, but I don't want to bend the
barrel, and I need you awake," I said, panting a little. "Can
you drive?"

"Man, I can't even see."

"If you can talk you can drive. You're going to do both."

"What about my gun?"

"It landed in a ditch with all the other hot iron in town. Turn the key." The engine had stalled.

"Where we going?"

"We're paying a visit to the Colonel."

He gave me a sideways look. His right eye had swollen almost shut. "Colonel who?"

"My line. That was who you were going to introduce me to tonight, wasn't it? The man to see about a fifty-caliber machine gun or a Polaris missile? Pesky private eyes disposed of while you wait?"

"Man, you must of hit me *hard*. I don't understand a word."

I grabbed a fistful of his shirt — another tank top — and rammed the muzzle under his chin. "Not as hard as if I use it the way it was designed. Drive."

He started the engine. I let go of him, pulled my door shut, and rested back against it with the gun propped on my knee while he swung the pickup back into the lane and headed deeper into the neighborhoods.

I said, "That was a military operation. Military operations mean commanders. What'd you tell him that made him put the bee on me?"

"Snuffings ain't my scene, man. What happened back there was a surprise."

"It was supposed to be. What'd you tell him?"

"What you said. You was a customer looking for heavy shit."

"A man who does business like that runs out of customers in a hurry. What else did you tell him?"

"Nothing."

"Shooter . . ."

"Okay, okay. He a man likes to axe questions. I said you a P.I. named Walker."

"Is that when he asked you to finger me, or did he do some checking and get back to you?"

"I didn't finger you, man."

"Shooter, Shooter," I said. "I won't cap you for setting me up. You get stuck in the middle, you take sides to live. Just don't insult me by denying it. That makes me angry. An angry man with a gun."

A blue-and-white passed us heading in the opposite direction, its lights and siren going. Its slipstream shook the pickup's rusty sheet metal.

"He called me back," Shooter said then.

"He say why he was taking me out?"

"Man, he didn't *say* he was taking you out. I just sell guns."

"Yeah, yeah. What's his name?"

He licked his lips. "Seabrook."

"Never heard of him. What's he colonel of?"

"I never axed him. He buys and sells."

"Did he do business with Doyle Thayer Junior?"

"I don't know."

"How about Waldo Stoudenmire?"

"Sturdy?" He grinned lopsidedly, favoring the right side of his face. "Sturdy don't know a butt from a trigger."

"Somebody taught him. Just before he died."

"Sturdy's dead?"

"That's what Ma Chaney said. Know anything about it?"

"Man, I hardly knowed Sturdy. We didn't have the same clientele."

"Sure you did. Doyle Thayer Junior."

"I don't know no juniors."

"Too fast, Shooter." A fire truck wailed past, one of the new ugly yellow-green jobs. "I don't care what business you had with him. I don't even know if Sturdy getting dead, if he's dead, has anything to do with anything. What I want to find out is what the Colonel thinks I know that's worth calling out the militia. Speaking of which, would they be the same four that's been knocking over houses in this area over the past couple of weeks?"

"My guess ain't no better'n yours. I never saw 'em before tonight."

"Shooter, you're going to die dumb."

"As long as I die old."

"You didn't sell them the automatic weapons they're using, that much I'm sure of. Ma did that. I saw the newspaper piece she cut out for her scrapbook."

"Ma pisses all over the lot. She don't care who she sells to."

"You do?"

"Fucking right. You never know when you might be doing business with a undercover cop."

"We'll ask the Colonel. We're still heading that way, right?" We had turned north on John R, where here and there a lighted apartment window hung like the last blossom of spring. The truck's tires sang on the dewy pavement.

"What you wanted," he said. "Man, you don't mind if I let you off early and tell you the way? I got to work in this town."

"I'm going in the front door and you're going with me."

"Shit. I had to ask."

"Where we going?"

"Ear-oh-quoyse Heights." He sang it. "Where the men wear sheets, the women are strong-smelling, and the cops are distinctly below market rate."

We skirted the edge of the city, following darkened streets past railroad yards, a string of cut-rate funeral parlors, and an oil refinery smelling thickly of crude, stopping at last near a weedy six-acre parcel enclosed by a chainlink fence. The sign said KEEP OUT.

"What's this?" I asked.

"City fairgrounds. This where they going to build their domed stadium." Shooter killed the engine.

We got out. Crickets stitched in the stillness. I put the revolver in my coat pocket with my hand on it. "You first, Kemosabe."

The gate was secured with a padlock and chain, but the narrow opening was no problem for a reedy type like the Shooter. For me it was a squeeze. Inside, the weeds were calf-high and wet; we hadn't gone five yards before our shoes began to squelch. As my eyes grew accustomed to the gloom, a long shape separated itself from the blackness surrounding it, a hangarlike structure with a shed roof and corrugated steel walls, eighty feet by twenty, without windows.

"Where they store the tents and stuff," Shooter whispered. "I think we beat 'em here."

"Not much of a front."

"The Colonel don't need one."

There was a small side door around the corner from the double bays on the north end of the building. Shooter tried the handle. It wasn't locked. I grasped his wrist as he was pushing it in. "Should it be?"

He shook his head.

I took the gun out and motioned him on. He mopped his palms off on his running shorts, set himself, and pushed the door open the rest of the way slowly. It swung silently on well-oiled hinges.

Nobody shot at us. I motioned again and he went in. I followed.

The interior smelled overpoweringly of mildewed canvas. I closed the door behind us, found my pocket flashlight, and flicked it on. Tented shapes loomed on the edge of the pencil beam.

"I think we alone." Shooter's voice, raised slightly above a whisper, echoed.

I said nothing. We were standing on a plywood floor in an aisle between what looked like stacks of crates covered with canvas, the stacks running the length of the building. They made gargoyle shadows on the walls. Once when I moved the flash abruptly, something squeaked and swooped past our faces with a wind of flapping wings.

"Bela Lugosi." Shooter covered his hair with both hands.

I found the edge of a canvas flap and jerked it back. Some dust flew up, not enough for something that hadn't been disturbed in months. I tested the lid of the crate beneath with my hands. It was nailed shut.

"Look for something to pry with," I said.

"*You* look. I didn't come here to do no hard physical labor." He sat on a covered crate across the aisle.

After a couple of minutes of poking around with the flash I picked up a three-foot length of broken two-by-four, inserted one end between the slats, and worked one loose with a shrieking of nails. I groped around inside the straw and came up with an olive-drab plastic object the size and shape of a hardcover book, only curved like a roof tile.

"What's that?" Shooter asked.

"Claymore."

"What's a Claymore?"

"Not your specialty. It's a portable mine."

"Mine!" He leaped up off the crate he'd been sitting on.

"If you say, 'Feet, do your stuff,' I'll shoot you."

"Better'n getting blowed to hell. I get there soon enough walking."

I set aside the Claymore and groped further, feeling around the edges of the others in the crate. I counted fifteen in all, enough to take out the building and some of the chainlink fence. Replacing the first mine, I pulled the canvas back farther. The next crate was longer, with coils of the same kind of straw sticking out between the slats. I bent down and sniffed. Then I straightened. "Smell it?"

Shooter stooped, inhaled. "Cosmoline?"

"Me too." Cosmoline is the pink gelatin they store guns in to prevent rust.

There were two more crates underneath that one. They were stacked three deep the length of the building. I was turning to say as much to Shooter when a shoe scraped the floor behind me and something tapped the mastoid bone behind my right ear. A white-hot bolt of pain shot to the top of my skull, followed by a wave of nausea, and after that nothingness had never seemed so good.

—— 15 ——

IT WAS ONE OF THOSE nightmares you kept waking up from, only to find yourself in the middle of another one just as bad.

For a time I floated naked in a sea of grotesque and vaguely erotic images. The stuff I was floating in was as warm as blood and slippery to the touch, but the air on my face was freezing, as if I had raised it from an ice bath and turned it to the wind. I tried to cry out, but my lips were stiff, and the sickly bleat that issued between them embarrassed me. Below the warm, slippery surface, blind sea-creatures slid past and between my legs, tickling the skin. The sky overhead was pink, like light coming through my eyelids.

Once — maybe more than once — the colors changed, from blood-red and fleshy pink to deep black, agonizingly cold and stinking of mildew, as if I had been swaddled in canvas and dumped into an open grave. This time I did cry out. Then again came the white-hot pain and the nausea, and as I sprawled backward into the bloody sea, two men spoke.

"Not so hard, Hube."

"Sorry, Jer."

At length — days or years, I was a man out of time — I emerged again into the mildew-stinking darkness, and this time I stayed. It wasn't as black as before. Somewhere at the edge of my vision a light glowed, a merciless shaft of naked incandescence I didn't dare look at because it would dry-cook my eyeballs in their sockets. There was a floor under my back. With the part of my brain that was working logically I knew it was plywood, and that the decaying smell around me was of the old canvas in the storage building on the Iroquois Heights fairgrounds. Deep inside my head a leaky faucet was dripping into an empty basin, the drips echoing hollowly when they landed.

Somewhere a voice made words that rang around the empty basin that was my brainpan.

"I suppose we should call an ambulance. His skull might be fractured."

"Naw. I got a hunch it's been cracked open so many times it's all bone collar, like when you break your leg and it knits stronger than it was."

"Well, he can recover in the infirmary in Jackson."

I recognized the voices. They didn't belong to the two men I had overheard earlier, or dreamed I had. Very carefully I moved my eyes. They grated.

The first man I saw was seated on the crate Shooter had occupied before, a thick man whose undershirt showed through the white shirt he had on over it with a narrow black tie hanging down in front and resting on his belly. A snapbrim hat clung to the back of his big curly head. A Cigarillo teetered on his lower lip.

When he saw me looking at him, Horace Livingood of the Bureau of Alcohol, Tobacco, and Firearms smiled his rubbery smile. "I bet you got a head the size of a garbage truck."

I said nothing. Victor Pardo's clean-cut face and unfashionably long hair moved into my vision, looking down at me a mile. The naked light was behind his head, one of a row of them strung along the rafters. "Can you hear me, Walker?"

"Yeah." My voice creaked.

"You have the right to remain silent. You have the right to an attorney. If —"

"Cut the crap," Livingood said. "We're just us." To me: "You up to sitting?"

"Sure. What am I doing now?"

He chuckled and got up to give me a hand. I grasped it, took a deep breath, and sat up. Someone swung a trash can into my face, but other than that it didn't hurt any more than chewing tinfoil. I touched the knot behind my right ear gently. It was sticky.

Livingood said, "Hit you more than once, from the look of it. To keep you under, probably. Whoever did it had practice. I don't guess you saw him."

I didn't answer. The place looked different, and it wasn't just the fact that it was lighted. The canvas on both sides of the narrow aisle lay on the floor, limp and deflated-looking. Except for a few obviously empty crates and one other thing, the building had been cleaned out. The one other thing was Shooter. He lay on his face at my feet with flies clotted on the back of his head. I noticed the sulfur smell then.

Resuming his seat, Livingood fished a plastic bag out of his coat pocket with my .38 in it.

"Yours, I guess. It was in your hand when we got here. Vic's got it all worked out. You shot the sorry son of a bitch, then sapped yourself a couple of times and hid the sap just before you passed out."

"I didn't say that. I said he should be arrested for questioning."

"How'd you wind up with it?" I asked Livingood. "This place belongs to the city."

"We've got someone in Dispatch at the police department. I got the squeal before the cars did. I shook Vic out of bed and we beat the dicks here. They're outside, limbering up the rubber hoses. I had a hell of a time quirting 'em back till our field men arrived to seal off the place."

"All for little me?" I was working on the nausea.

"I like you, but not that much. We've suspected for months that someone's been dealing weapons out of the fairgrounds. When we tried to set up surveillance, Cecil Fish — you know him? Thought you might — got a court order warning us away. Elections coming up, can't have *federales* snooping for contraband on city property. Anyway, when we heard there'd been a killing here, we put on our running shoes."

"Who tipped the cops?"

"Somebody named Anonymous, who else?" He slapped the empty crate he was sitting on. "Looks like we were wrong; no weapons here."

"What time is it?"

"Little after five. Sun'll be up in an hour."

"Five hours ago you could've fought a war with Ohio from in here," I said. "The place was full of Claymores and rifles packed in cosmoline."

"You can still smell it. No wonder they had to keep sapping you down; it's a big operation. Wonder if anybody in the neighborhood heard the trucks."

"Who would they report it to, the cops?"

Livingood was watching me. "I'm not so sure Vic isn't right — about questioning you, I mean, not the other. You wouldn't still be breathing if somebody with a lot more imagination than brains didn't get cute and try to set you up for the Shooter. Thing is, we've been on this a year and couldn't get any farther than the front door, and here you are sitting in the middle of it after only two days."

"Lucky me." I stood up, caught my balance, and swallowed bile. To avoid bending down, I used my foot to nudge a section of canvas over the dead man's upper half. The flies buzzed around angrily and lit on the canvas.

"Being a little guy has certain advantages," I said. "Nobody thinks I'm worth a court order."

"Better stretch it some. You're running short."

"It felt short." I patted my pockets, found the crushed pack of Winstons, and shook one out. I still didn't have a match, and Livingood wasn't volunteering. I held the cigarette by its ends with my thumbs and forefingers and looked at it. At least I was still seeing single. "Shooter brought me here to meet someone named the Colonel."

"Colonel what?"

"Seabrook, he said. Ever hear of him?"

"Maybe."

"We found the place unlocked with nobody in it. I was just starting to look around when the lights went out. Mine."

"Still short." He was admiring the Smith & Wesson in the clear plastic.

"That's as much as I know. The rest is pure guesswork."

"Guess."

"This Seabrook party thought I was getting close to I don't know what. He had Shooter bring me here, sapped me down, did him, and tipped the cops so I'd roll over for the kill."

"Kind of hard on the Shooter."

"Maybe he'd outlived his usefulness."

Pardo said, "Why do it here, if it meant giving up safe storage and clearing out the inventory?"

"It wasn't safe storage," I said. "You knew about it. A federal judge might overturn the local court order anytime, and even if he didn't, the city would pull its support once the elections were over. Now was as good a time to move out as any. Odds are they've had another warehouse lined up for some time."

"What makes you so dangerous?" asked Livingood.

"If I knew that I wouldn't be standing here nursing a headache."

"It doesn't scan." He rubbed his face for a moment, then reached behind his back and tossed a pair of handcuffs at my feet. "You better put those on."

"You're kidding."

"Mister, I'm holding the murder weapon with your prints on it and those are my bracelets on the floor. When Washington hears about the one they're going to ask why I didn't use the other. I don't hear anyone laughing."

"About time," Pardo said.

I crushed the cigarette into a ball and threw it away. "Okay."

Livingood said, "Okay?"

"Okay, you win. This one wasn't planned, at least not by someone with the brains and cash to arrange this whole setup. It was jury-rigged on the spot by a grunt who thought he'd make points with the boss. The real job was supposed to take place last night in the warehouse district in Detroit, where four men with machine guns did some body work on my car. I was supposed to be in it at the time."

The senior agent rested his hands on his knees. "You kind of forgot that part."

"No law says I have to report an attempted murder on private property to federal authorities. Having fingered me, it was the least Shooter could do to offer me a ride here. The rest you know."

"Four men with machine guns."

I nodded. "I made the same connection."

Pardo said, "What?"

Livingood ignored him. "Too cheesy. What's Seabrook doing messing in armed home invasions?"

"You tell me. I never heard of him before last night."

"If you're lucky you won't hear of him again. But I doubt it."

"Who is he?"

"Classified," Pardo snapped.

"Shut up and listen, Victor. You might learn a thing or two about police work." Livingood dropped his Cigarillo and squashed it underfoot. He never had lit it. "He's an honest-to-Christ lieutenant colonel, or was until the marines washed him out after that thing in Grenada. Seems he shot a second lieutenant in the leg when the looey didn't hit the beach fast enough to suit him. There'd have been a court-martial, only Washington was taking enough heat over the invasion without it, so they let him resign his commission. It was either that or a Section Eight.

"He turned mercenary after that, which I guess is what you do when you're born an army brat, graduate West Point, work your way up from first lieutenant, and they take away the uniform. Seems he'd been dealing military ordnance to the private sector for some time before he shot that second looey — the marines unwound that one a little late — and he used the profits to set himself up in business: buy guns here, sell them there, and finance armed expeditions to Africa, Iran, Central America, all those hot places where people got nothing better to do on a Saturday night than put on camouflage and knock over the government. Bureau wants him bad. We were hoping to turn something on him in Doyle Thayer Junior's basement after the rich little bastard got dead, but the man covers his tracks. Munitions are hard to come by in these numbers. I don't think he'd be dumb enough to waste any of them on a string of glorified B-and-E's in his own backyard. What if a gun got left behind and the cops traced it to whatever armory it was stolen from?"

"Maybe he didn't use his own guns," I said.

He jumped on it. "Is that another guess, or you got something to share?"

"Just a guess." I shoved Ma Chaney's clipping out of my thoughts. Cops like Livingood have been known to read minds. "Say he had something big in the hopper and needed a lot of money in a hurry. He couldn't sell off some of his weapons without drawing attention to himself, and anyway maybe he needed them for the big thing. He could rob a bank — he's got the men for it — but that's daylight work, someone might get caught and blab. Instead he knocks over some well-to-do homes when the residents are in and there's no chance he'll trip a silent alarm. It means going in heavy. Any way you read those invasions they sound like a commando raid."

"He'd need a fence."

"Around here he'd have his choice." I got rid of Sturdy Stoudenmire as quickly as Ma's newspaper clipping.

"So what's the big thing?"

"Ask Shooter."

He looked at the corpse. "Poor old Shooter. How do you suppose he got tangled up with the big kids?"

"Sometimes the small fry get large ideas. Sometimes it works out. More often they wind up floating in formaldehyde down at County."

"Words to live by." He was looking at me now. He took my gun out of the plastic bag and held it out. "In case you can't swim."

I took it. "What's it going to cost me?"

"The usual. You turn something, you don't run to the locals with it. Here's my card." He produced it from a leather folder. I holstered the .38 and put the card in my wallet.

"He's a smoking gun!" complained Pardo.

Livingood stood up with a grunt. "The work's hard enough without doing the city cops' job for them, Victor. Especially in this city. Even if murder was our lookout, nobody ever shot anybody and then cold-cocked himself repeatedly."

"Maybe he's got friends."

"If they were any friendlier he'd be feeding the flies just like Shooter." He looked at me again. "You need doctoring?"

"What I need is a drink."

"We'll give you a lift as far as Detroit. You can walk from there and join the crowd waiting for the bars to open."

"What about the cops outside?" I asked.

He flicked aside the canvas covering Shooter with his foot. "Must leave things as we found them. No telling how much time they'd waste looking for a hitter polite enough to throw a wrap over the mark."

"Is there a Lieutenant Romero out there?"

"Which one's he?"

"The one who looks like a young Gilbert Roland. He's hard to bluff."

"He's not there. They all look like Sydney Greenstreet, just like every other bent dick I ever met." He picked up his handcuffs and put them away. "Let's go, Ironskull. I'm expecting my wake-up call any minute."

— 16 —

THE WEEDY LOT was awash in the glare of police cruiser spotlights and the inevitable rotating red and blue beacons. Garbled voices came over two-way radios cranked up to full volume. Once outside, Livingood put on his Fed face, flashing his shield around the group of uniforms and plainclothesmen — they smelled of cigars and cheap after-shave, like cops everywhere — and making material witness noises in my direction. Pardo said nothing, a vote in his favor. Livingood kept us moving as he spoke and before the cops could work up the impetus to stop us we were in his unmarked Ford rolling toward the opening in the fence.

"Bolt cutters," he said, when I asked him how there came to be an opening. "Field agents and second-story men shop at the same stores."

I had him exit the expressway at a Ramada Inn north of Detroit.

"Taking the day off?" He stopped under the canopy and

switched off the ignition. The sun was breaking red over the scattered cars in the lot.

"It's Saturday," I said. "I don't feel like spending it talking to the Detroit cops about my broken car."

"You're lucky. Washington doesn't recognize Saturdays." He rested his elbow on the back of the seat. I was sitting next to him with Pardo in back. "What about that drink?"

"I was just kidding. I'd rather sleep."

He popped open the glove compartment and handed me a pint of Southern Comfort.

"I did deep cover in 'sixty-nine with the White Panthers in Ann Arbor," he said. "I got the shit kicked out of me once and there wasn't anybody to offer me a bottle. I've carried one ever since." He started the car. "You've got my card."

I waved at him from under the canopy.

The clerk at the desk, a Japanese girl in a gold blazer and ruffled blue blouse, looked at my rumpled clothes as I was filling out the registration card. "Sir, do you have luggage?"

I patted the pint in my pocket and smiled. She shoved the key at me.

There was an ice machine at the end of my corridor. I filled the plastic container from the room, skinned cellophane off a glass, and poured Southern Comfort over the cubes. It tinted them pale orange, like the sun as it cleared the window. The room was large, with twin beds, a big bath, and a terrace overlooking the parking lot. All the rooms in the motel were the same size. I was in the mood for a fly-blown little cell with a dusty bulb and a bed with springs that sounded like a Vincent Price movie, but the nationwide chains have just about made them extinct. They've eliminated the worst along with the best and left us with the middle ground.

I felt greasy under my clothes. I took off my shirt and shoes and worked my toes in their damp socks into the carpet. It felt cool from the air conditioner. In the bathroom I ran cold water onto a washcloth, gingerly scrubbed the blood from the lump behind my ear, held the cloth to the back of my neck for a moment, then to each of my wrists. Then I washed my face and looked at it in the mirror. Finally I went back out for my drink. It tasted sweet, the way Southerners liked their liquor and their women, or so I was told. I'd never been there. The world was full of places I'd never been. Vietnam didn't count. Working in Detroit most of my adult life, I felt like a spinster who'd wasted her youth taking care of an invalid parent. Except spinsters hardly ever woke up on their backs in empty buildings on deserted fairgrounds with their heads pounding and dead men at their feet.

Stop complaining, Walker. You made your choice the day you stepped off the plane carrying your duffel and turned right toward the office of Apollo Investigations and not left toward the post office, where they give the civil service exams.

Things were starting to fall into some kind of order. Colonel Seabrook had pulled off the home invasions for case dough to finance some operation or other. Ma Chaney had sold him the weapons so he wouldn't have to dig into his own stores. Shooter's part was still smoky, but selling guns he would cross the Colonel's path from time to time; maybe he had smelled something and cut himself in. Sturdy had been fencing the items taken in the home invasions, and was killed for one of two reasons: Either the Colonel had all the money he needed and was covering his tracks or, more likely, Sturdy had gotten hungry and tried to arrange a partnership. My poking around put me on the clean-up list. It was the easiest case I'd ever solved. Now all I had to worry about was the one I'd been hired for.

I finished my drink, stretched out in my clothes on one of the beds, and slept without dreaming.

*

I woke up at three, hungry and not sure where I was. When I remembered, I called the desk and asked for room service. The clerk, a man this time, said there wasn't any but recommended the motel coffee shop.

A copy of the *Free Press* lay outside my door. I took it with me to the coffee shop and went through it over a steak sandwich and a glass of water. The fairgrounds killing was on an inside page in a column of late-breaking stories from the greater metropolitan area. There were no names, just a paragraph saying a body had been found. There was nothing in the paper about Sturdy. I finished eating, paid, and had the clerk call for a taxi from the desk.

It was another steamy day, but there was a dark fringe of clouds in the west and by the time the cabbie let me off at my house it had cast its shadow over the entire west side. Thunder trundled in the distance.

The house smelled like a freshly opened Egyptian tomb. I left the door open, flung up all the windows that weren't painted shut, and stood under the shower for fifteen minutes. When I came out I wrapped a towel around myself and plugged in the telephone. I caught it in mid-ring.

"Where the hell were you all night last night and all day today?"

"John?"

"Answer the question," Alderdyce said.

"As good as can be expected, John. And how are *you*?" I sat down in my towel and crossed my legs. It was growing dark out now, although it was barely four-thirty. The wind was coming up.

"I'm fine, you're fine. Everybody's fine. Your car's sitting by the river with more holes in it than a fleet of Buicks. You want to tell me how it got there?"

"Gasoline."

"Say that again, you son of a bitch."

"John, I never knew you to get so worked up over a car."

"Witnesses heard automatic fire and the pattern of the

bullet holes bears that out. I'm investigating a series of crimes involving men armed with automatic weapons. You'll excuse me for getting worked up when I find out you've been standing this close to the mouth without tipping me."

"Quite a jump."

"I'm in shape for it. How about you? Any holes to match the ones in your chassis?"

"None."

"Good, good. You going to come down here and make a statement or do I have to send out the Huns?"

"What if my car was stolen?"

"Come down and file a complaint."

"What if I do?"

"I'll stuff it down your throat."

"I didn't think inspectors did that kind of thing."

"That kind of thing is what got me made inspector. What about it?"

"I'll be there in an hour."

"Make it a half hour."

"I might be thirty minutes late."

"Then your story better be thirty minutes better."

"I'm on my way."

"Thought you might be. Oh. About your friend Sturdy."

"Yeah." I felt my fingers cramping on the receiver.

"We picked him up for questioning this morning. He's in Holding with a bad case of the sniffles, but that's as close to dead as he's been lately. You better check your sources."

"Maybe I'd better." We stopped talking to each other.

=17=

THE DOORBELL RANG while I was sitting there thinking. I wasn't expecting anyone. I had turned on the
lamp beside the chair when it had grown dark. Now
I switched it off and went to the door in my towel with the
Smith & Wesson in hand.

Constance Thayer said, "Is that how you dress on
weekends?"

"The artillery is optional." I put it down on the table by
the door. "Come in and sit down while I go put on a hat."

"You don't have to on my account."

I let that one slide and closed the door behind her. She
was dressed a lot more casually herself, although casual for
her was another woman's idea of dressing up: long-sleeved
black-and-white checked blouse tucked into tailored char-
coal gray denims with a crease you could cut your finger on
and white sandals with two-inch heels over stockings. Her
reddish hair was teased into bangs on her forehead and tied
into a loose ponytail behind her head. She looked seventeen.

"You're a tidy bachelor," she observed.

"I'm never here long enough to mess it up."

A long crackling peal of thunder uncoiled directly overhead, rattling all the crockery in the house. She jumped straight into my arms.

Immediately she put a hand against my chest to push away. It stayed there. She was wearing sandalwood.

"I'm sorry," she said. "I guess I'm a coward after all."

"Just two clouds bumping together." We separated. "I'll be back in two minutes."

It was nearer five. I went at my beard with the scraper, combed my hair, and put on a sport shirt, slacks, and loafers. This time I left the Brut in the medicine cabinet. I found her sitting on the sofa with her legs crossed, smoking. She had switched on the lamp. Rain was clouting the west side of the house. I closed a window on that side and asked her what she was drinking.

"Nothing today. I'm in danger of becoming a lush."

"Who isn't?"

She was staring at me. "Are you all right? You look like you've been in a fight."

"I thought I left all that in the shower."

"It's just a look you have."

"Technically it wasn't a fight," I said. "He had my body but he didn't have my soul. I guess you're here for a progress report."

"I hope you don't mind. My sister is a wonderful woman, but I can only spend so much time with her before I have to strangle her or get out. All this sitting around waiting is hell. When there was no answer again at your office I looked you up in the directory."

I sat down in the easy chair. "Your husband did business with some heavyweight bad guys. A woman with three sons doing time or about to be and a Mongoloid top hand with a hearing aid is the best of them."

"So you have made progress?"

"It depends on what you call progress."

"Now you sound like Leslie."

"You're right," I said. "No, I haven't. I got off on a tangent. It's a common hazard. Cecil Fish will challenge Dorrance to prove in court that Doyle did anything more incriminating than buy an occasional gun from the crowd I'm talking about, and he won't be able to. That's all Doyle did."

"It might be enough, if the crowd is as bad as you say."

"Maybe. More probably I'm wasting your money."

"It isn't worth anything to me if I go to prison."

Lightning lit up the dark window, turning the street outside into something etched on tin. I waited for the answering clap, then: "Did you tell Dorrance about the money and me?"

She nodded. "He threatened to withdraw when I told him I'd re-hired you."

"Threatened?"

She smiled.

"Okay, you've still got Dorrance. I'll give him what I've got. He can do what he wants with it."

"You're not quitting."

"Not because I got knocked around, if that's what you're thinking. It's part of the life, like getting busted when you pick the wrong pocket. Whichever way I go from here will just take me farther away from what you hired me to do."

"But you can't know that until you follow it to the end."

"Call it a feeling."

The rain was coming harder now, yammering on the roof and smearing the windows. The air smelled of iron oxide. She had to raise her voice.

"Please don't give it up. I've got so few people on my side."

I didn't feel like shouting. I left the chair and walked up to the sofa and bent over her.

"Buy a calendar, lady. The Middle Ages closed out of

town. The moat's a duck pond and they sell souvenirs in the tower. Prince Albert's in a can, the convent's a Wendy's, and horses run in the money or they feed the dog. This year's big hero is a cartoon rabbit. I'm on your side because you paid me to be."

Our faces were closer than when I'd had my arms around her. She lifted hers and closed her eyes and I kissed her.

When it was over I went back to my chair and sat down. She opened her eyes and gave me the look. "What happens now?"

"The sun will come out. It always does. Then it will get hotter."

"It always does," she said. "I mean, what about us?"

"That noise you heard was thunder."

"I didn't hear it. What are you grinning at?"

I stopped. "Summer re-runs."

"What?"

"I knew a P.I. once, young guy and pretty good-looking, thought he was the best thing to happen to women since pantyhose; broke hearts like the rest of us break shoelaces. He disappeared one whole winter, and some of us thought he'd eeled his way inside some rich widow's garter belt and gone to Texas. Everyone was going to Texas that year. Then spring came and the Ferndale cops found what was left of him stuffed into a culvert with his handsome face battered in and eleven dollars in his wallet. They arrested the woman a month later in San Francisco. Seems he'd been working for her husband and took pictures of her in a motel with the husband's business partner. She found out and offered to fall in love with him if he tore up the pictures. Which he did, knowing women couldn't keep their hands off him and that any double-cross she might be planning would go out the window once she had a taste of him in bed.

"Turns out she and the partner had been emptying the till for months and had bought two tickets to California and a leather briefcase to carry the cash. While she was keeping the P.I. occupied, the partner shot the husband as he was working late in the office, cleaned out the safe, and rigged the place to look as if somebody had broken in. When she got the all-clear call, the woman hung up and hit the P.I. a couple of dozen times with the telephone. The partner showed up in the company station wagon, they ditched the body, and took off for a more agreeable climate."

Mrs. Thayer said, "I bet there's a moral."

"No matter how good you think you look, there's always someone or something that looks better. And I'm not nearly as good-looking as he was. A couple of times a year someone tries to convince me otherwise, usually when I have something they want or am doing something they don't want me to do or am not doing something they wish I would. Sex is the closest thing we've got to a nickel on a string; you can spend it all over town and still have it to spend. I'd rather have a drink. It's already paid for when you get it."

"If you feel that way, why did you kiss me?"

"I said I didn't trust it. I didn't say I gave it up."

She took her cigarette out of its tray and broke off the ash. "I guess I deserved some of that. But I'm not a whore. When Doyle was charged up on booze and pills, the only way I felt safe with him was during sex. It got to be a weapon of self-defense. Once it becomes a tool, well." She took a last drag and put out the cigarette. "The rain's letting up. Thanks for the shelter."

I watched her get to her feet. "I'll stay with it a little, see where it takes me. I'm not making any promises."

"Do you ever?"

"Not often. They're not a renewable resource. When you let one go it should count."

She nodded. At the door she paused. It had grown lighter out and the runoff from the roof was the loudest sound, gurgling through the gutters. "Was that a true story?"

"Most of it. They didn't kill the husband. The money wasn't that big."

"What about the private eye?"

"He was practicing in Flint last I heard, bedding the occasional city councilman's wife in return for favors. The business partner broke into his office and stole his file on the case with all the pictures and negatives while the P.I. was sleeping with the woman. He woke up with a hangover was all. I thought the part about having his face bashed in was a nice touch. The object lesson is the same."

"I like it better the way you told it."

"Most people do. There has to be a murder in it."

"What does that say about people?"

I moved a shoulder. "We're still evolving."

She went out, leaving behind a faint trace of sandalwood.

After a while I called for a taxi and went out too. I gave the driver an address in Macomb County.

THE RAIN HAD COOLED THINGS a little after all. A damp breeze stirred the leaves on the trees along Cheyne and the sun shone in a scrubbed blue sky. We detoured around a couple of fallen limbs and cruised slowly through a puddle that stretched from curb to curb and covered the cab's hubcaps. Somewhere a chainsaw spluttered and soared into a high-pitched snarl.

The house in the country didn't look any more lively than it had the day before. It hadn't rained there; the grass was the same burned-out amber and dust lay thick on the burdocks near the road. I told the driver to wait and went up and rapped on the screen door. No one answered.

The door was hooked from inside. Placing my body between it and the cab, I took out my pocket knife and ran the blade up the jamb. The hook sprang out of the eye with a little tinkle.

The living room hadn't changed, except now a glunky lamp with a fringed shade occupied the table where the forest fire had stood. Ma or someone else had swept up the broken glass and thrown it away. There was a tiny half-bath under the stairs that had been a broom closet, and another door led into a fair-size kitchen with an old-fashioned white gas stove and a refrigerator, newer and avocado colored. No bodies tumbled out when I opened the door. The last person to leave had locked the back door behind him.

Upstairs I found two bedrooms and a full bath. One of the bedrooms contained a single bed with a painted iron frame and a cracked nightstand with a drawer full of thumb-smeared magazines with girls in black panties on the covers. This would be where Hubert Darling had slept. The closet was empty. The other bedroom had to be Ma's. The double bed had a flowered coverlet. A lamp with a lace shade stood on a nightstand with claw feet and a brass ram's head you had to grab by its nostrils to slide out the drawer, which contained a carton of Marlboros and a Bible as old as Gideon. The wallpaper was blue with pink cherubs. The closet was jammed with frilly polyester nightgowns in every color and shade, kimonos like the one she had greeted me in yesterday and worse, and six pairs of bib overalls. A cheap dresser with family pictures on its top — Emma and Calvin and four towheaded boys posed in front of vintage automobiles — held king-size lacy underdrawers and men's flannel shirts in Ma's size and a gray metal strongbox under a stack of pillowcases.

The box was locked. I set it atop the dresser, found two hairpins, and sprang the lid after fifteen seconds. Inside were the title to a brand-new Ford Blazer, four brown and curling birth certificates, letters from various penal institutions bound together with a green ribbon, and two deeds. One belonged to that house and lot. The other contained a description of a sixteen-acre parcel in the northeast corner of the county. The street address was included. I took it down in my notebook, returned the deed to the bottom of the box, locked it, and put it back where I'd found it.

That was the inventory. The letters from Ma's sons, labo-

riously written in soft pencil on lined sheets, read like post-
cards from summer camp and had been mailed as much as
a year apart. Nothing about the house said that she had ever
traded in anything more lethal than peach cobblers. Livingood had said she was a good deal smarter than her boys.

When I climbed back into the cab, the driver set aside his
crossword puzzle and rested a thick freckled arm with a
kewpie doll tattooed on it across the back of his seat. "Where
to now, bub, the big square dance?"

I said, "Let's avoid the rural humor and find a town and
a place that rents cars."

"I'm sorry, sir. I can't rent you a car without a credit card."

The rental agent was a short blonde with a flat face and a
gray silk scarf around her throat. The tag pinned to her
jacket read MITZIE. Behind her was an alphabetical rack
filled with tan envelopes with lucky renters' names block-
printed on them in black marker. Posters of happy couples
gliding along in sleek convertibles plastered the walls.

"How big a deposit do you need?" I asked. "I brought
enough for the down payment on a new Lincoln."

"I'm sorry, sir."

"Okay. I sent away my cab. How about a lift to the nearest
stand?"

"Sorry, sir. I can't leave the counter."

I was the only customer in the place. I shared it with her
and a mechanic in blue coveralls taking a cigarette break in
the corner. I monkeyed around with that for a moment, decided Mitzie wouldn't appreciate what I had to say, and
headed for the door. The mechanic stepped out of the corner. "I think I can help you, Mac."

I put my hands in my pockets and faced him. He was a
square-shouldered piece of work with no waist and a
smudge on his long jaw. His brown hair was cut short with
a natural wave in front.

"You heard me say I had cash on me, right?" I asked.

He smiled in a way that reminded me of Livingood. "If I was to turn mugger, I wouldn't start with you."

"Okay."

The blonde was glaring at us. He blew her a kiss and opened the door for me.

We walked around the building and through a side door with a carburetor propping it open into the garage, where a concrete floor tilted down to a drain at the back. A new Olds Calais was up on the hoist and three other cars were parked along the sides, two with feet sticking out from under them. The third was a gray Mercury, a square boat with hideaway headlamps and bumpers like construction girders. We stopped in front of it.

"How old?" I asked.

"Let's just say it remembers Vietnam." He leaned in through the open window on the driver's side and popped the hood latch. I opened it and whistled.

"V-8 Continental Mark IV," he said, using a rag to rub a spot of grease from a gleaming half-acre of engine. "The pollution equipment's a dummy. Speedometer goes up to a hundred and twenty, but she'll do twenty over that easy. I bought it off a dope dealer who needed bail money. Get a load of this." He reached through the window again and heeled the horn ring. Twin blasts flattened the air, one slightly out of pitch with the other. They sounded like air raid sirens.

"Jesus Christ, Harley." In the ear-splitting silence that followed, one of the other mechanics sat on his dolly rubbing a fresh lump on his bald head.

"Sorry, Ed."

I asked Harley about the transmission.

"Put it in brand new when I overhauled the engine. The boss says I got to get rid of the machine. I don't have a garage."

"How much?"

"Six-fifty."

"Why so cheap?"

He smiled again, drew a screwdriver from one of his coverall pockets, and swiveled the plate bearing the serial number aside from the engine block. There was a different one underneath, stamped into the block itself. "The Dade County Sheriff's Department is looking for it down in Florida, or they were," he said. "The insurance company paid off and tacked another penny on its rates. Everybody's happy." He screwed the plate back in place.

"What about a title?"

"I found the same make and model totaled out in a junkyard up north and bought the title. Then I stamped the plate. The numbers match."

"I'll take it." I started counting bills out of my wallet.

"Don't you want to test-drive it first?"

"No time. I believed what you said about not starting with me."

He stuffed the money into his screwdriver pocket, took the title out of the glove compartment, signed the back, and gave it to me. "What business you in?" he asked.

"I trace stolen cars for the FBI."

He turned white.

"Just kidding," I said.

"You son of a bitch."

The big Mercury swooped along the straightaway and sat on the curves like a boulder. When I floored the accelerator, the steering wheel jerked my arms straight and the stench of scorched rubber stung my nostrils. In no time at all the needle buried itself on the right side of the speedometer. The AM radio had a tinny speaker and the cigarette lighter didn't work, but the big frame rode the bumps and potholes like heavy silk. The engine rumbled, making the soles of my feet tingle. I ran the dial up and down, but there is never a Beach Boys tune playing when you want one.

Dusk was smoldering when I left the pavement and tore

down a gravel road hauling a column of dust behind me. A big doe bounded across in front of me once and I threw two wheels up on the bank to avoid hitting it, nearly losing control when they bit into soft earth. After that I throttled down. Tree limbs met overhead in a tunnel effect, turning the road into a cathedral. Mine was the only car on it.

The address on Ma Chaney's deed belonged to a fieldstone farmhouse standing alone in a field that hadn't been plowed since Hoover. Wild alfalfa had grown over the foundation of a barn forty paces away that had long since burned or been torn down to decorate someone's recreation room. A navy-blue Chrysler sedan I thought I recognized stood in the rutted driveway behind a dusty green Blazer.

As I approached along the road, a blossom of gray smoke opened in one of the house's empty windows and the Chrysler's sideview mirror exploded. A man hunkered at this end of the car in a camouflage jacket and pants leveled his weapon across the rear fender and returned fire. The report chattered.

The chattering was repeated on the other side of the house, but it wasn't an echo. I spotted more smoke and another camouflage jacket just above the barn foundation. Another report from the house, and the window on the driver's side of the Chrysler disintegrated. At that range a shotgun is as effective as an automatic rifle, but whoever was in the house was hampered by the Blazer parked in between.

The man by the Chrysler rose into a low crouch. When the firing started up again from the ruins of the barn, he charged the house, cradling his rifle. I punched the accelerator and leaned on the horn.

Howling like a fleet of squad cars, the Mercury bounded into the field, headed straight toward the charging man. He stopped, whirled, loosed a stream of bullets — one of which squealed off the Mercury's windshield frame — and leaped out of the way.

I didn't try for a second pass. I wheeled wide around the house, bumping over old corn stubble, and fumbled the Smith & Wesson out of its belt holster. The ornament on the hood was shaped like a gunsight and I made use of it, aiming the car straight for the empty foundation and the man crouched behind it. At the last second I yanked the wheel hard right, stretched my right arm across my chest with the gun in my right hand, and fired through the open window. I aimed by instinct rather than sight and squeezed the trigger until the hammer snapped on an empty chamber.

I threw the revolver down on the seat and used both hands to wrench the wheel as far as it would go to the right. The Mercury plowed the field in a tight circle and lurched into the ruts it had made on its first pass, but I needn't have bothered. The man was standing in plain sight on this side of the foundation, bent over with both hands clutching his abdomen. His rifle, snout-shaped with a black plastic banana clip and a collapsible skeleton stock, lay on the ground at his feet. I drove over it deliberately.

Now for his partner.

No luck there. He had recovered himself and scrambled back into the Chrysler, and as I swung around the house he backed into the road and took off with a roar and a hail of flying gravel. I gave chase for a country block, but I had lost momentum on the turn, and when a lumber truck trundled into the road in front of me out of a narrow logging trail, taking up both sides, I turned around and went back to the house.

Just as I stepped out behind the Blazer, a wind buffeted my left side and something stung my hip like a cluster of yellowjackets. Then I heard the roar of the shotgun.

"Stand right there or the next one takes your head off, you Yankee trash," called Ma Chaney from the house.

═ 19 ═

B OY, YOU GOT TO LEARN to sing out," Ma said. "I could of blowed you out of your shoes."

It had taken some talking to convince her I was friendly, and then some more before she would come out and help me drag the man I'd shot into the house. She was wearing a man's corduroy jacket on top of her overalls with the sleeves turned back and a man's felt hat jammed down over her orange hair. The shotgun, an aging Ithaca pump with a scarred and dented stock, never left her hand.

The farmhouse wasn't as neglected as it appeared from the road. The roof was new, and although the north wall had collapsed into rubble, someone had erected a substitute out of cement blocks. The ground floor was stacked to the ceiling with kegs of gunpowder and boxes of ammunition and C-4 explosives. It wasn't as impressive as the Colonel's store in Iroquois Heights, but it was enough to turn the house into a crater if a spark were struck.

I said, "You picked a swell place to hole up during a firefight."

"Ma didn't pick it; they did. I was supposed to meet the Colonel here, but when them two boys piled out packing auto-rifles . . ."

There was no furniture in the house. We laid the wounded man, panting and semi-conscious, on the floor in the front room and I tore open his blood-slicked shirt.

Ma tsk-tsked. "Gutshot?"

"Not quite. There's a rib or two shattered, though." I pulled off his olive-drab beret and stuffed it into the hole to staunch the flow of blood. He was not more than twenty-five, with clean features and dark hair with an Oliver North cut. I didn't know him from the President's podiatrist. He had no identification in his pockets.

"Right good shooting," Ma said, "from a moving car."

"I was just throwing lead."

"How'd you know who to throw it at?"

"I figured that Blazer out front belonged to the title I found in your strongbox. That put you inside. And I was pretty sure I saw that Chrysler last night when my car got shot up. Besides, I don't like automatic weapons." I sat back on my heels. "He needs a hospital."

"Use the phone."

It was standing on top of an open crate of shotgun shells.

"Why didn't you call for help?" I asked.

"Anytime Ma can't handle two pups with squirt guns, she'll learn needlepoint."

I lifted the receiver and dialed 911, grunting with the effort. She pointed at the bloodstain on my slacks. "You're hit."

"I picked up a few shotgun pellets. I wonder whose." When the operator came on I told her a man had been shot and where to send the ambulance.

"Get them pants down," Ma said when I hung up. "You got a pocket knife?"

"Those are two sentences I hoped never to hear in that order."

"You want to get infected?"

"Every time we meet you try to get me to strip." I fished out the knife, undid the slacks, and dragged them down my hips. She left the room. I heard water running. She returned with a damp towel, a wad of clean rags, and a bottle of Aqua-Velva. She put the rags and the bottle on the crate I was sitting on and used the towel to sponge away the dried blood from my leg. The three pellets were blue-black under the skin.

Ma opened the knife and poured Aqua-Velva over the blade. "My boy Mason's after-shave," she said. "It's the only thing here with alcohol in it. Hang on to something."

I gripped the crate with both hands while she probed and pried. I sweated a little.

"Okay." She cleaned off the fresh blood, splashed stinging liquid into the holes, and wound one of the clean rags around the leg. "You better see a doc later. Ma ain't no nurse."

I pulled up the slacks and fastened them. "Sorry about the inventory. The cops will seize it."

"Can't without no warrant, and it'll be long gone by the time they get one. Ma knows some folks."

I knelt by the wounded man and pried up both his eyelids. There was no talking to him that day. I sat back, looking at Ma. She had turned on a light finally. Outside the frogs were singing. "What happened?"

"What I said. I had an appointment with the Colonel. I got this."

"What was your business with Seabrook?"

She got a sly look on her face. She had sweated in streaks through the thick powder and it wasn't pretty. "So you know him now. Who's asking, you or the *po*-lice?"

"I shot a man today and I want to know why. Maybe you owe me."

"Well, like I said, Ma didn't need you." She shrugged.

"He wanted to buy some guns. Said he'd meet me here."

"Any idea why he sent in the troops?"

"If I did I wouldn't of agreed to meet him here."

"Where's Hubert Darling?"

"The little sneak cleared out yesterday while I was visiting my boy Wilbur in the hospital in Ypsi."

"I think he's with the Colonel now."

"What makes you think it?"

"Just a nightmare I had. What about Sturdy Stoudenmire?"

"What about him?"

"Yesterday you said he was dead. Today the Detroit police have him in custody."

She shrugged again. "I heard a bad rumor."

"Who told it to you?"

She got the sly look again.

I said, "I know you sold Seabrook the guns his men have been using in the home invasions. What do you think they were shooting at you with? Now that he doesn't need you he's mopping up, knocking over anybody who might tell the law what he's up to. You don't owe him anything."

"That never was Ma's long suit anyway." She heaved a porcine sigh. "It was one of the Colonel's boys. He come to make a pickup, never mind what. I knew he was from the Heights so I asked him what he heard from Sturdy. 'Sturdy's dead,' he said. Ma said, 'When?' 'Tomorrow night at the latest,' he said. That was Tuesday."

"What's this big mouth's name?"

"They never use names except the Colonel's. Wasn't this fella." She nudged the man on the floor with the toe of a brogan several sizes too big for her. Ma liked to kick them when they were down. This one groaned and stirred but didn't open his eyes.

"Maybe Sturdy outsmarted them," I said.

"Sturdy couldn't outsmart a sock."

"Then he's got something the Colonel wants."

"Like what?"

Far away a siren separated itself from the *chee*-ing of the frogs. "Let's ask him," I said. "What's the Colonel's number?"

"What are you going to say to him?"

"I'll make it up as I go."

She gave me the number. After two rings a smooth masculine voice came on the line.

"Yes."

"Colonel Seabrook," I said.

"Who's speaking?"

"Is this the Colonel?"

"This is Winston Seabrook." He sounded more youthful than expected.

"This is Amos Walker," I said. "I'm out at the farmhouse. I just shot one of your men. I didn't like him."

There was a very short pause.

"I think you're mistaken. I've retired from the military. I don't have men."

"Yeah, well, this man you don't have is bleeding all over my shoes. I'll need a new pair."

"Explain."

"Ask Sturdy."

"I don't know anyone by that name."

"Nobody does. That's what being in jail will do for you. I'm his new partner. You'll be doing business with me while he's indisposed."

"And what sort of business will we be doing?" He sounded amused.

The siren was growing louder. Others had joined it. I stuck a finger in my exposed ear and raised my voice.

"Not over the telephone. Tomorrow's Sunday. I'll be in my office Monday morning at eight. Don't bother sending your men to my house in the meantime; I won't be there.

Come alone, and bring double what Sturdy was asking."

I cradled the receiver. Ma seized it. "I better call for the truck now," she said. "Them laws'll truss me up with this shooting till they get the warrant."

"Who are you calling, Mason?"

She hesitated with her finger in the dial. "I don't know where Mason is. Neither does the FBI."

"Ma, they're going to bury you cagey."

"Listen to the skunk telling the muskrat he stinks. What you fixing to do when the Colonel finds out you ain't got what he wants?"

"Maybe by Monday I'll have it. A lot happens on weekends."

She snorted and dialed. "Hello, Mason?"

I put a hand on my throbbing leg and waited for the cavalry.

=20=

I T WENT TO A sheriff's investigator named Galvin. After the man I'd shot had been whisked away and a paramedic from a second ambulance crew had patched up my leg, a company of sheriff's deputies took Ma and me in separate squad cars to the county building in Macomb, with two more deputies following in the Mercury and Blazer. I was parked in a ballroom-size conference room to deal with my agoraphobia alone until Galvin came in.

He was a stumpy Scot with a big head, small delicate hands, and tired brown eyes with a slight cast in the right. I had known other cops with that feature, and it was always an advantage to them; you never knew precisely where they were looking. His suit was a brown sack and the tip of his red tie peeped out of the bottom of his vest like a cat's tongue when it's cornered something. He put his hands in his pockets and stood at the opposite end of the long conference table.

"Anybody read you your rights?"

"A kid in a uniform mumbled something," I said. "You ought to check them for baby teeth before you swear them in."

He gazed out the window — I think. It was a moonless night and all he had to look at was the lighted parking lot a floor below. "That young man you shot might not live."

"That young man was trying to shoot an old lady. You recovered his assault rifle."

"It was broken. It could have been a discarded item from the farmhouse."

"I broke it when I ran over it. By now you've matched the tread marks to my tires."

"You overestimate the efficiency of our lab." He took his hands out of his pockets. "That old lady has been selling guns and explosives illegally since before my father came over from Edinburgh. I can't tell you how long we've wanted her here at County. I suppose we should be grateful to you for that."

"You don't sound grateful."

He produced a plastic bag — how cops got along before plastic is one for the Durants — and dumped its contents out on the table. I recognized my wallet and notebook and a familiar crumpled pack of Winstons among the loose change. My gun had been sent to Ballistics. He drew a silver pencil from an inside pocket, poked among the items with the eraser end, and flipped open the wallet, exposing my investigator's ID and honorary star from the Wayne County Sheriff's Department.

"What's a private cop from Detroit doing in my county?"

"Motoring. I didn't see your name on the sign when I crossed over."

He tipped back the notebook cover with the pencil and looked at the first page. "Shorthand." He let the cover fall shut. "Who are you working for, or is this one all for yourself?"

"It's not shorthand. Just poor penmanship."

"There's more than a thousand dollars in your wallet. You always carry that much cash?"

"You should've seen it a few hours ago."

"You never really answer a question, do you?"

I didn't answer.

"Why'd you shoot him?"

I tilted my head. "Until a lawyer walks through that door, I didn't shoot anyone."

"Mm-hm." He tapped the pencil twice, then flipped it onto the table. "This would be a good place to live if you Detroiters would crap in your own can. We're booking you for assault with a deadly weapon and if the man dies we'll make it murder one. Then when the search warrant comes through we'll tack on possession for sale of explosive materials and conspiracy to violate the Sullivan Act. That ought to be good for life."

"That's seven years in people years."

His errant eye fixed on my left ear. "It doesn't have to be seven months."

"Make your pitch."

"Give us Emma Chaney."

"Make another."

"I'll fix it with the D.A. Probation, maybe, if your record's clean. Six months if it isn't, unless of course you're wanted; then it gets complicated. But we can knock off something."

"What if the D.A. won't play?"

"You think I'd offer you a deal I hadn't discussed with him?"

"Mm-hm."

He looked at the ceiling — I think. "Suit yourself. When we shake loose that warrant we'll have enough evidence to put you both in denim for years."

"So why are we talking?"

Someone knocked on the door. He went to it, opened it

far enough to stick his head out, then opened it the rest of the way and stepped outside, closing it behind him. I heard voices raised in the hallway, then silence, a lot of it. He came back in looking as if someone had died owing him money.

"You had your phone call?" His voice was steady. I hadn't noticed that before. It meant he was working at it now.

I said I had.

He picked up the silver pencil and used it to push my effects farther down the table. "Put this stuff back in your pockets. They're here."

"Both of them?"

"A fat one and a skinny one, and they don't answer to Stan and Ollie." He watched me stand up and stretch and come over to claim the items. Satisfaction glittered in his normal eye at my stiff-legged walk. "I wish to hell you Feds would call someone before you bulled your way into local jurisdiction."

"I'm not a Fed."

He said nothing more and we went out into the hall, at the end of which Agent Pardo was standing looking out a window covered with steel mesh — it overlooked the same parking lot — and Horace Livingood leaned against a wall smoking one of his little cigars. He stayed where he was as I approached. "You get in trouble when you're alone."

"Sorry I got you up again," I said.

"Sleeping's for civilians anyway."

We stood around not talking until Galvin stumped off. Livingood watched him go.

"Sociable sort, ain't he?"

"Leave him alone. You'd be the same way if the rules changed on you suddenly."

He nudged his hat farther back. I figured he started the day with it square over his eyebrows and when it finally fell off he went home. "Feeling sorry for the cops now, are we?"

"I'm too tired to be a rebel. Where can we talk?"

"We can see people coming a long way from right here. Victor there can sing out if anybody tries shinnying up the drainpipe."

Pardo grunted.

I said, "The man I shot belongs to Colonel Seabrook. You'll want to find out what hospital they took him to and have men there in case he wakes up. He and one other were shooting at Ma Chaney when I got to the farmhouse. She doesn't know why, only that she was supposed to meet the Colonel there. The other one got away in last year's Chrysler." I gave him the license plate number. Pardo wrote it down in a notebook with an alligator cover.

"How'd you know about the farmhouse?" Livingood asked. "We didn't."

"I found the deed when I broke into Ma's place."

"Aren't we enterprising."

I let that one blow. "The sheriff's men recovered the wounded man's assault rifle at the scene. One of the victims of the home invasions might identify it, if not its owner. The invaders wore ski masks."

"We'll let the locals put that one together. We want the Colonel for international trafficking in illegal weapons, not penny-ante burglary."

"That penny-ante burglary has netted him over a hundred thousand so far. Investment capital for the big thing we were talking about this morning."

Pardo was looking at me. "Why are you so cooperative all of a sudden?"

"I owe you something for the spring." I kept my eyes on his partner. "I've got a client with a short court date and I can't spare the three days it would take to do this by the numbers. That's why I called you. I thought if the material witness scam worked in Iroquois Heights it would work here."

"It can be overdone," Livingood said. "What else?"

I told him about Hubert Darling and the possibility that he'd gone over to the other side. I didn't mention Sturdy Stoudenmire or the call I'd made to the Colonel. Pardo took down Darling's name. Livingood finished his Cigarillo and threw the butt in a corner, where it smoldered on the linoleum.

"Let's you and me head back to the office, Vic. We'll set up the checkerboard and wait for Walker to call us when it's over. I don't know why we didn't think of it before." He sounded bitter.

I said, "I'm not trying to do your job. It happens my job and yours keep crossing trails. I work my own hours, so sometimes I get there first. No one will be gladder than me when we get rid of each other."

"Don't bet on it," he said. "Let me tell you something about nets. They're not real discriminating. There's always some little fish that get drawn up in them along with the tuna. If they're spotted early enough they get thrown back, but usually they end up in a big smelly pile on the dock where they rot. It's too bad, but it's one of the risks you take when you swim with the big fish. Let's go, Vic."

After they left me I found my way to the property clerk, a blunt-faced lifer in his sixties, who shoved a receipt at me for my valuables and informed me my gun was being held for evidence pending dispensation of the case. I signed the receipt, asked him about my car, and was directed to the ground floor, where I waited in line at another counter and got a voucher from a fat woman in a sergeant's uniform to show to the attendant at the impound. In the lobby I used a pay telephone to call Detroit Police Headquarters. The party who answered said Inspector Alderdyce had gone home. I tried his home number.

"Funny you should call," he said. "I saw your picture on a milk carton in my refrigerator."

"Sorry about today, John. Something came up."

"You better be calling from headquarters. Otherwise I'm putting your description on the radio."

"I can't make it this weekend."

"Try."

"I'm staying low. But if you send a couple of men to my office Monday morning at eight-thirty, I'll hand them the man behind the home invasions."

"Be specific."

"I just need one favor."

"I'm fresh out of favors. I ran out this afternoon."

"I need this one before I can hand over the man I'm talking about."

He seemed to sigh. You can't really tell over the telephone. "Feed it to me."

"Hang on to Sturdy at least until Monday. If he walks this weekend the whole thing goes to hell."

"Too late. We kicked him three hours ago."

"What for?"

"Something called the Bill of Rights. The public defender kept waving it at us, and since we didn't have anything on Sturdy we thought it might be nice to humor him. Now, what —"

"Sorry again, John." I broke the connection.

I needed a gun. I'd left my Luger in the Chevy and it would take a degree in Civics to pry the Smith & Wesson loose from the Macomb County Sheriff's Department before Christmas; I hoped their relationship with the police in Iroquois Heights was as bad as all the others' in the area, and that no effort would be made to match the gun to the bullet in Shooter's brain. I'd done the cops' job for them too well, getting one of the only two quickie gun merchants I knew killed and the other arrested. I chewed over it on the way to the garage and while I was standing in another line waiting to take my car out of hock. Then I remembered something.

I almost ran over a deputy while spiraling the Mercury

down to ground level between the rows of sheriff's cruisers and confiscated automobiles. In the rearview mirror I saw him unholster his sidearm just before I turned the corner into the street.

It was a slick night, high and moonless, with the stars bright pinholes in the circle of sky and the county roads — those newly blacktopped, anyway — deep black ribbons under the headlamps. From time to time a pair of turquoise-colored eyes would gleam in the light, then vanish into the weeds at the side of the road. It was just past midnight when I crossed the Wayne County line and made tracks for Detroit. There the streets were still wet from the afternoon rain and reflections crawled on their surfaces. The air smelled scrubbed and sweet.

I drove straight through to Jefferson, encountering only one red light on the way. Some nights are like that. There were no police barricades at the warehouse district, just a smattering of shattered glass that had been swept up against the base of a building to glitter in my headlamps. The Chevy had been towed away. From there I traced the route Shooter and I had taken in his pickup toward the spot where I'd roughed him around. I hoped I could find it. More than that, I hoped no one else had.

I found the intersection, left the Mercury at the curb, and descended the slight bank on foot holding my pencil flashlight. The grass was shoetop-high and wet, soaking through my socks and plastering my pantscuffs to my ankles.

After ten minutes of searching I was about to give up when the beam of the flash found something that gave back light. I turned over a soggy square of corrugated cardboard that had been a discarded carton, jumped back when something scurried out from underneath, then stooped and picked up Shooter's nine-millimeter Beretta from the spot where it had landed when I had tossed it out of the pickup. I wiped off the grass and dirt with my handkerchief and kicked out the clip. It was loaded for bear.

$$=21=$$

WALDO STOUDENMIRE LIVED, or had lived when last I'd had reason to look him up, in a hotel for permanents and transients in a neighborhood in Iroquois Heights that had started out as carriage trade, deteriorated, come back, and had begun to decline again. There were some elegant old homes in the area that had been kept up through the determination of older residents who remembered better days, next to houses with plywood in the windows, cars up on blocks on the front lawn, and nightly screaming matches inside conducted in murky Middle Eastern tongues. The place could go either way from there.

The lobby would have been larger and more ornate in other times. Now it was a narrow passage flanked by mustard-colored wallboard with a desk at the end and a sallow middle-aged party in a green plaid jacket snoozing behind it. That kind only wakes up when it hears a suitcase dropping out a window. I helped myself to a pack of matches with the hotel's name printed on it from a dusty bowl on the desk and took the stairs. The yellow leaf carpet runner was worn a quarter-inch down and a foot across.

Sturdy's room was on the third floor next to the elevator, which didn't have a car anymore and had been used as a garbage chute for years. When nobody answered my knock I slipped the latch with the edge of my investigator's license.

The room was small and neat, like its resident. A stack of racing magazines occupied the lamp table next to the single bed, which had been made and turned down with a maid's meticulous routine, even though the hotel didn't have one. The rug was a patch of bright color on the noisy floorboards, cheap but clean. Three inexpensive suits hung on wooden hangers in the closet, over a pair of black shoes and a pair of brown shoes with hard rubber heel- and toe-plates on their soles and wooden trees inside. Each of the suits' inside breast pockets contained a small comb. The dresser yielded nothing of interest. Sturdy lived as if he expected a cop with a search warrant three times a week. Where he kept the goods he fenced depended on which township wasn't holding an election that year.

The window was nailed shut, with paint on the nailheads. The panes were nearly opaque with soot and squinted out on a fire escape coated with orange rust.

The only item in the room that had cost anything was a new portable color television set on the dresser. It was still warm. I hit the power switch, then hit it again quickly when a re-run of *The Untouchables* sprang on, rat-a-tat-tatting at top volume. Whoever had been watching last liked noise.

There was a bath and a door that connected with another room. I opened it, but the facing door was locked on the other side. I stepped into the bathroom. It had been done in black and white deco the first time it was in style, with a few broken tiles now and a wave in the mirror over the sink that made my face look like something in an aquarium. The toilet was white with a black lid. The white enamel tub was a nice long one you could stretch out in if Sturdy weren't there already.

He was fully dressed in a neat tan poplin suit and a pair of two-tone saddle shoes floating on their heels on top of the water. His paisley necktie was floating too, but his face was under the surface with his thin brown hair drifting out around it and his eyes and cheeks puffed out as if he were still holding his breath. His skin was the gray shade of cooked liverwurst; at least that hadn't changed. There were puddles on the floor next to the tub and his fingers were cramped around the rim on both sides. I tried prying them loose and gave up.

I leaned back against the sink, poked a cigarette between my lips, and lit it from the fresh pack of matches. I smoked it down to the filter, flicking the ashes into the toilet, then dropped the butt in after them and flushed it. I watched until it went down. Then I rolled up my sleeves and got down on my knees and went through Sturdy's pockets.

He didn't have much, just the usual comb, forty-eight dollars in soggy bills in a small brass clip, two flat tablets in foil, and a slim pocket pad with a blue plastic cover and a gold pen clipped to it. No wallet or keys; Sturdy didn't drive. Many of the earlier notations in the pad had bled through and were illegible, but the water hadn't soaked through to the pages in the middle. I shook it off, wrapped it inside my handkerchief, and pocketed it.

The tablets looked familiar. They were plain white and the foil was unmarked. I got up and checked the medicine cabinet. There were more of them in a brown plastic bottle with a white snap-on cap and a label with a doctor's name and "nitroglycerine" typed on it.

It could have been a break, although not for Sturdy. If he had a bad heart and it gave out before whoever was holding him under could obtain the information he was after, I might still be in the game, whatever the game was. If so, the killer was either too disgusted to remember to search him, or too stupid to consider it. All things being equal, in the latter event I had a fair idea who he might be.

Someone banged on the hall door, loudly. "Police! Open up!"

I left the bathroom and checked the window. Someone was standing in the alley under the fire escape. Through the soot and darkness, stray light from the lamp on the corner lay on an oval of metal on his chest.

"Open up!" The door bucked in its frame.

I snatched a penknife and a collar pin from atop the dresser and inserted them in the keyhole of the locked connecting door. The tumblers were worn smooth and hard to grip.

"Give me that passkey."

The passkey was rattling in the hall door lock when my lock gave. I stepped through the connecting door and drew the other one shut behind me, pushing the lock button, just as several pairs of heavy feet thudded into Sturdy's room.

I was in a bedroom like the one I had left, except this one was a lot less neat. My feet tangled with clothes on the floor and the air smelled of ashtrays in need of emptying. The room was dark, but an oblong of dirty light coming in through the window fell across a figure sprawled on its back on top of the bedcovers, a figure vaguely female in an old-fashioned white slip with a pair of pantyhose bunched up on one leg. A lot of hair ruthlessly peroxided and punished into waves like bent brass lay on the pillow. The woman was snoring ecstatically. Under the ashtray smell I detected a bellyful of gin and the kind of perfume that ought to come in big jugs with diagonal red stripes on the labels.

I had taken the Beretta out of my belt just in case. Now I returned it and mounted a search for the source of the gin smell. From the timbre of the snores, I wasn't going to be interrupted.

The bottle had fallen off the bed, probably out of the

woman's hand, and rolled to a stop against one of the legs, where the carpet was damp around it. When I picked it up, its contents settled into a cozy half-inch on the bottom. I carried it into the bathroom, shut the door, and switched on the light over the sink. The layout was black and white like the one in Sturdy's bathroom, but that was where the resemblance ended. The floor was shaggy with strands of blond hair with gray roots and the sink was green with mold. Tentacles of wet pantyhose dripped from the overhead rail into the tub, where several varieties of mushrooms thrived. The toilet tank was a jungle of bottles, atomizers, and jars of industrial wrinkle cream. A pyramid-shaped bottle half full of the perfume I had smelled in the bedroom wore a tag around its neck with a handwritten message: "For Corinne from her favorite sniffer. Love, Andy."

The bathroom was separated from Sturdy's by a common wall. Excited voices murmured on the other side over the body in the bathtub. I took a swig from the gin bottle, and as the heat climbed my spine I shook the remaining drops into my palm and smeared them over my neck. For good measure I sprinkled some of Andy's perfume onto my shirt. I checked the goods in the mirror, decided I looked too upstanding, rumpled my hair, and unfastened two shirt buttons. Now I looked like the tattered end of a gaudy night and smelled like a Sunday sermon.

Corinne was still rattling the plaster when I left the bathroom. Just as I turned my back on her she stopped in midsnort and started whimpering. I went back and got the empty gin bottle and pressed it into her hands. Without opening her eyes — they looked painted shut, like the windows — she turned over on her side, raised the bottle to her lips, and started sucking on the neck. Very soon she was snoring again.

I left her. The idea was to get to the door before they started banging on it and woke her up. I took a deep breath, then opened it and leaned against the jamb, shaking loose my last Winston.

A uniformed officer with a twisted nose and the general look of having been broken down from sergeant at least once turned around at the noise and stared at me, fingers resting on the butt of his revolver. I hoped he hadn't been among the group at the fairgrounds last night.

"What's the argument?" I said sleepily. "Can't a guy hang over in peace in this burg?"

"Who're you?" His voice sounded like a circle saw turning on reduced current.

"Andy Winters." Wintersong was the name on the perfume label. "If you cops busted these hookers on the street where you're supposed to, you wouldn't have to wake up honest citizens."

"What makes you think we're arresting a hooker?"

"Isn't the mayor running again in November?"

"You got identification says you're Andy Winters?"

I shook my head. I got the cigarette lit finally. That hadn't entirely been an act.

"Nothing? No driver's license?"

"They took it away in April."

"You live here?"

"Corinne does. I'm a friend."

His mud-colored eyes flicked past me. "That Corinne?"

"It better be. I don't sleep with strangers these days."

"What's Corinne's last name?"

I grinned moronically and shrugged.

"No strangers, huh." His fingers stroked the revolver's butt like a cat kneading its claws. "Where you from, Winters?"

"Why the grill?"

"Answer the question. They passed an ordinance in this town against cohabitation in nineteen-oh-three. I could run you in on it if I had a mind."

I didn't touch that one. "I live in Harper Woods."

"You walk all the way from Harper Woods?"

"Corinne drove. We went out."

"Smells like you had a good time. Where'd you go?"

"I don't want to get anybody in trouble."

"Blind pig, huh? When'd you get in?"

I scratched my jaw. "Eleven, eleven-thirty."

"Which is it?"

"Eleven-thirty, I guess."

"You hear anything the last hour or so?"

"You mean besides that?" I tilted my head in the direction of the racket on the bed. "What happened, somebody get rolled?"

"You know who lives in three-ten?"

"Corinne might. If you can wake her up. I gave up nudging her finally and got dressed. I don't suppose you cops could call me a cab."

The desk clerk from downstairs joined us. He looked awake now. He had small suspicious eyes and a V-shaped mouth with no lips, like the flap of an envelope. Awake or asleep, his skin was the color of bad buttermilk. I had him down for alcoholic hepatitis.

"You know this guy?" the cop asked him.

He stared at me hard and shook his head. Then his nose twitched. "We might as well just take the door off its hinges. I'd of gave her the boot a long time ago, but she's paid up till January. Two-bit whore."

"That's my girl you're talking about," I said.

"This guy says he came in with the lady around eleven-thirty. You see it?"

He was still staring at me. "Nobody came in at eleven-thirty. I been on duty since eight."

"And asleep since nine, I bet," said the cop. "What is it, Flask?"

The newcomer was a uniform at least fifteen years younger than the other, with a ginger-colored puppy moustache and sergeant's stripes on his sleeves. His eyes were on me.

"He says his name's Winters, Sarge. He was sleeping next door, he says."

"Has the lieutenant seen him?"

"No."

"Get him."

Moving like someone with strong opinions about taking orders from cops two-thirds his age, Officer Flask left us and went into Sturdy's room. He returned a minute later with Lieutenant Romero.

═22═

H E HAD TRADED his cocoa straw hat for a narrow-brimmed Panama, cream-colored with a black silk band and beautifully blocked. The rest of him, except for his brown face and hands and polished black shoes, was blue: a midnight blue suit and a navy blue knitted tie on a powder-blue shirt with the collar buttoned down. His narrow Latin face was solemn as always. The black eyes betrayed nothing, not even recognition. He looked at the officer.

"You found him where?"

"Right here, Lieutenant. It was sort of he found me."

Romero looked at me again. "Do you make it a habit to always attack the thickest part of the fence?"

"It was a judgment call." I knocked off some of my ashes. "Naturally I didn't expect you to be working this shift."

He nodded. When he spoke again, his intonation hadn't changed.

"Cover him, Sergeant. Officer, brace him and search him for weapons."

Flask hesitated only briefly. He had his sidearm out before the young sergeant could react. "You heard him, Andy. Against the wall. Pretend you're doing pushups, only standing. Spread the legs."

As I turned, the sergeant drew his revolver finally. Flask kicked my feet apart. I had to grab the wall to keep from falling. My cigarette dropped to the floor. He patted me down swiftly, found the Beretta stuck inside my belt under my shirt, and stepped back.

"How'd you know, Lieutenant?" he asked.

"See what else he has on him."

I was relieved of wallet, keys, and Sturdy's notepad wrapped in my handkerchief. I had left my own notebook in the car.

"Well, what do you know for asking?" Flask said. "He's a private eye named Walker. And he's loaded."

"Give them here. Cuff him, Sergeant."

The younger cop hooked cold metal around my left wrist, yanked it behind my back, and cuffed the right. I turned around. Romero had the Beretta in one hand and my wallet and Sturdy's pad and the keys to the Mercury in the other.

The sergeant spoke. "Think he's our man, Lieutenant?"

"Maybe. Stoudenmire wasn't shot."

"I told you he didn't come in with the tramp." Triumph glittered in the desk clerk's nasty little eyes.

"Thanks for your help," Romero said. "We'll call you."

The clerk pouted, but it didn't work without lips. "You won't tell the papers the name of the hotel. I like this job."

"Nobody but you cares." Romero waited.

The clerk bent to pick up my cigarette, stamped out the smoldering carpet runner, and retreated toward the stairs. The lieutenant went on waiting until the steps stopped squeaking. "What happened, Walker?" he asked then.

"It was love at first sight. I mean Corinne and the bottle."

"You're not talking to the chief now."

He sounded a little hurt. It was too far past my bedtime

to wonder if it was a trick. "Do we need the Praetorian Guard?"

He thought about it. "Officer, secure the front of the building," he said. "Sergeant, call downtown, tell them we need the medical examiner and a wagon. Use the telephone in the lobby. The print men are late as always."

"Procedure is two men with a suspect at all times," the sergeant pointed out.

"I've read the manual, too."

The sergeant moved his shoulders around disapprovingly, touched his moustache, holstered his gun, and started stairward. I made a chirping whistle in his direction and half turned, wriggling my fingers.

Romero said, "Take back your cuffs, Sergeant."

"I just put them on."

"That was for the clerk."

"Procedure —"

"I'm sure you'll tell Chief Proust all about it. He's paying you enough to spy on me."

He unlocked and removed the cuffs more roughly than he had applied them and took them downstairs. Flask handed me one last muddy glance and followed.

Romero tapped on the door to the room opposite Corinne's with the Beretta's barrel, waited, tapped again. When no one answered the second time, he produced the passkey and opened it. He motioned me in first.

It was a dusty front room with a bare mattress on an iron frame and the shade drawn over the window. The Cuban turned on the overhead light and closed the door behind him, double-locking it. There were no chairs in the room. I sat on the mattress. "Where's your other half?"

"Pollard? We're not joined at the hip." He laid my things on a child's-size writing desk with a skin of dust on top and put his hands in his pockets. Waiting.

"Who hollered cop?" I asked.

"A woman in the building. She tried calling down to the clerk to complain about the loud television in three-ten and when he didn't wake up she called us. I recognized the room number; Stoudenmire spent more time downtown than the night cleaning crew. I thought it was worth a look. It was."

"Whoever turned up the volume did it to cover the noise when he drowned Sturdy," I said. "If he drowned. I found heart medicine in his pocket and in the medicine cabinet."

"I guess that's when your pants got wet." It was an invitation.

"I got a bad tip a couple of days ago that he was dead," I said. "When I heard he was alive I came here to ask him how come. Then you showed up."

"Who told you he was dead?"

"Emma Chaney."

"I don't know her."

"She sells guns in Macomb County, or did until the sheriff's men picked her up tonight. She will again. She said she heard it around," I lied.

"What does Stoudenmire have to do with the Thayer killing?"

"That's the other thing I came here to find out. Ma Chaney did some gun business with Doyle Thayer Junior. Sturdy recommended her and gave young Thayer a letter of introduction."

"I heard you were off that case."

"I was for a while. Now I'm back on."

"Sort of like Billy Martin."

"The money's smaller," I said. "Are we going downtown or what?"

"Should we be?"

"If you're planning to charge me with breaking into Corinne's room. You'll need a motive to prove murder."

"Who has one?"

"Strictly speaking, nobody. I think he died on whoever was trying to soak information out of him in that bathtub. The autopsy will show if his heart gave out."

"That could have happened while he was drowning."

"Only if there's water in his lungs. If there isn't we're in business."

"Are we."

"You've got his notebook. I'm holding the other cards, or at least some of them. What's it worth to a cop in Iroquois Heights to solve the biggest case his town's seen in years, right out from under the federal government and the Detroit Police Department, and in an election year to boot?"

"Stoudenmire isn't that big."

"That's not the case I'm talking about."

He took a lacquer box from his inside breast pocket, removed one of his long slim cigars, and set fire to it with the gunmetal lighter. Blue smoke turned in the stale air. "Mrs. Thayer has confessed to killing her husband," he said, watching it. "Thayer Senior wants her convicted quickly and with as little noise as possible. The policeman who stirs things up won't be a policeman long."

"Not here. You don't want to be an Iroquois Heights cop your whole life."

"Sometimes it seems like I already have been." He blew a series of rings. "I was hired through Affirmative Action. When I placed first in the sergeant's examination they had to promote me from uniform or look bad. I made lieutenant last year when I broke an auto-theft operation involving three states and all the television stations in Detroit covered it; there was an opening and they couldn't very well ignore me. But I make Proust worry. An honest policeman who is very good at his job is always a threat to policemen like Proust. He has people watching me on duty and off. I have to be very careful. Other officers may fudge the details. Not Romero, or he's out. Unemployment doesn't pay enough to buy my family's freedom."

"A detective's post with a real police department would."

"Maybe. A man may take chances, but not with his wife and daughters."

I stood up. The air was getting thick and the cigar wasn't Cuban. "I'm not talking about the Thayer killing, either. I mean the armed home invasions that have been taking place in the area over the past two weeks. And maybe something behind them, much bigger."

He rested the cigar on the edge of the writing desk. "I'm listening."

I told him it, all of it, starting with the attempt on me in the warehouse district where I had gone to meet Shooter and ending with my telephone conversation with Colonel Seabrook. He didn't interrupt me.

"I wondered about that shooting at the fairgrounds," he said when I'd finished. "That one went to Schiller. When Schiller was with Narcotics, he was the one they sent down in the sewer to catch the drugs when the suspect flushed them."

I said, "He's still pulling the same duty. Shooter kept his ear to the ground so much it had roots. I figure he caught wind of the Colonel's action, probably the home invasions, and dealt himself in. Seabrook played him a while, then jerked him when he had the time to do it. The sloppy way his killer tried to frame me says it was the same hired hand who killed Sturdy and didn't think to search him or his room. Sturdy had something the Colonel wants. Whatever it is it costs, because after pulling in a hundred and ten grand from the robberies he still hadn't enough to buy it. When I declared myself a partner I forced his hand. I didn't know then that Sturdy was out of jail. You could say I got him killed."

"He set himself up when he got hungry. Maybe he talked before he died. That would explain why there was no search."

"In that case we're out of luck."

"You keep saying *we*."

"I'm being rhetorical."

"Like hell you are." His Castilian reserve was beginning to flake off.

"If you were going to do this by the numbers you wouldn't have taken me in here."

"You read much into people you don't know."

"So do you. We're trained to."

He showed his teeth in a grin for the first time since I knew him. It wasn't a pleasant expression.

"The system is the same everywhere. They teach you the job and then they won't let you do it. Wherever I go I'm still a *peón*."

"Not if you won't be one."

"You were born with that attitude. It's not so simple for me."

I said nothing.

He poked among the items on the desk. At length he picked up the notepad, balanced it on his palm for a moment as if weighing it, and held it out, still wrapped. "Your handkerchief, I think."

I took it. "What are you going to tell the others?"

"I don't have to tell them anything. I'm the ranking officer on the scene. Wait until the morgue crew gets here before you leave. I'll have different uniforms downstairs by then." He opened the door.

"Can I expect you Monday morning at eight-thirty?"

"I'll be free." He went out into the hall and closed the door behind him.

═23═

W HERE DO YOU GO when you're asleep on your
feet and you can't go home?
The system has an answer. You can go to a hotel,
motel, an inn, or the mission, where you're advised to sleep
with your shoes on lest you lose them to a roach who wears
your size. The hotels have room service, the motels have
vending machines on every floor, the inns have country
charm in bales, including antique bedpans which if you're
caught using one you get tossed out on your bladder. You
can get a single room or a double, or maybe a suite with a
refrigerator and a cabinet stocked with liquor in little plastic
bottles like the airlines sell, with a door that makes a cash
register ring somewhere every time it's opened. You can get
poolside, outside, no side; a corner room by a busy elevator
or a shoebox between the ice machine and a room full of
AA dropouts having a party; single bed, double bed, queen
size, king, where you need a compass to find your way out
and no reminder — if you ever needed one to begin

with — that you're all alone in a bed that could sleep a family of Cuban refugees. (I had Cuba on my mind for some reason.) Closed-circuit television, cable television, or just television, but always television, except in the fleabags; and even some of them have radios, connected to the baseboards with cables as thick as your wrist. The big chains equip the bathrooms with moisturizers and shampoos. The mom-and-pop places hang Handi-wipes over the sinks in place of towels and washcloths. The fleabags have no private bathrooms, just a community closet on each floor with a sink, a toilet, and a shower, and no lock on the door in case somebody hangs himself from an exposed pipe.

There are as many kinds of places to stay as there are people to stay in them, and every one of them smells to varying degrees of mildew and suitcases and daylight sex. If you strung out all the neon from all the motels on all the strips in all the cities of North America you'd have enough to wrap the world twice around in a glowing pink tube with some left over to twist into script reading VACANCY for the benefit of weary interplanetary travelers — but they'd better bring their own soap, because you can lose one of those toy cakes in an armpit. At every hour of every day and night someone is on his way somewhere, and everyone needs a place to sleep. I was in the wrong business.

I wound up in the same place I'd stayed the day before. It was the same room, although the number on the door was different and it was on a different floor. Everything was the same, except this time I didn't have a bottle for a roommate.

That was deliberate. The local Meijer's was open twenty-four hours. I'd bought a shirt, pants, socks, a change of underwear, a jacket to cover the gun, and a razor, then stepped into the supermarket section to buy a roast beef sandwich at the deli counter. The liquor section was next to it and I thought about it, all those lovely bottles in provocative shapes with attractive labels and contents ranging from liquid-diamond transparency to golden amber; but when liquor starts to look better than a woman's calf or a frisky pup, one drink leads to eighteen, and I couldn't afford to lose all of Sunday. I got a pint of milk instead. Aesthetically there was no comparison.

I ate the sandwich in the room and washed it down with milk over Sturdy's notebook. It wasn't any use. Even the dry pages were starting to blur. I considered a long bath, but kept seeing Sturdy in the tub, so I showered off Macomb County and Iroquois Heights, put on the clean underwear, and turned in. I dreamed Sheriff's Investigator Galvin was trying to drown me in a glass of Southern Comfort. I didn't seem to be struggling too hard.

Four hours later I shaved and dressed and brought a steaming Styrofoam cup back with me from the coffee shop and tried again. Late-morning sunlight was canting in through the glass doors leading to the balcony. I was clean and rested and the headache was better, but what I was reading didn't make much more sense than it had before I went to bed.

The first six pages were stuck together, and when I got them apart finally I was looking at indecipherable smudges. The last half of the pad, and the dryest, was blank. This left eight relatively legible pages covered with Sturdy's neat round schoolboy script. The notations weren't coded, but they might as well have been. They consisted of a series of surnames followed by numbers that might have been times, possibly of appointments. I recognized the name of a well-known local Lithuanian antique dealer — there couldn't be two walking around in the area with a mouthful of letters like that — and two or three others, more common, that were shared by bric-a-brac retailers in and near Detroit. None of it meant anything in a court of law, although considering Sturdy's trade it raised some questions about their legitimacy, as what else was new. I didn't figure it was worth killing him over. One name in particular caught my eye, both because it appeared to be a Christian, not a last, name, and because it was underlined. The number following it was 10:07. Whether it was A.M. or P.M. and what date it was for had gone to rest with the man who had written it. Myrtle was the name.

It could have been something. It could have been just a name in a book. That's the trouble with real life. You never know what pieces belong to which puzzle.

I started with the obvious. Leaving the room key in the ashtray for the maid, I cranked up the gray bomb and burned some gasoline visiting the furniture and antique dealers whose names I'd recognized. It was a balmy Sunday and they were all open for business. Of the four I spoke to, one had heard of Sturdy, but would never, never do business with him. Two more, the Lithuanian included, had no time for me as soon as they found out I wasn't shopping for furniture. The fourth, a tall woman leaning hard on fifty with eyeglasses hanging from a chain around her neck and hair dyed brittle black and combed into crisp waves, said she didn't know anyone named Stoudenmire and invited me into the back room to convince me. I declined.

Some of them were lying, of course. The antique trade in non-tourist towns is a paying hobby at best and if it's going to be even that you have to do some business with your eyes closed, just like every other shoestring industry forced to operate in a state with a crazy single-business tax. But none of them knew anything about what Sturdy was into when he was killed, and I was pretty sure none of them had killed him. If I was wrong I'd be back. After you've eliminated the impossible, whatever remains, however improbable, must be the truth — unless you were a little too hasty the first time. For now I was back to revving my engines on the runway with no place to fly.

The last shop I'd been to, the woman's, was a Queen

Anne house in Hazel Park, around the corner from a pancake joint smelling of hot grease and flour in the waitresses' hair. It was full, and while I was waiting for it to thin out I bought the late edition of the Sunday *News* from a stand on the sidewalk out front. When a booth opened up I ordered coffee and a short stack and read the article about the body in the bathtub in Iroquois Heights. It was a sketchy three inches and neither Lieutenant Romero nor I was mentioned. Two lines at the end said that no services were planned, according to the deceased's sister, Hilda Stoudenmire Myrtle.

═ 24 ═

MOTIONS.
Going through them is what the work amounts to most of the time. You scratch up a lead and tug at it until it breaks loose and dumps you over backwards, then you get up and start scratching again. Each lead might be the magic one that takes you all the way to the prize, and the minute you forget that and expect it to be another dud it comes to life and sinks its fangs in the back of your hand. It's just as true that if you behave all the time as if you're on to something hot you burn out early. Either way you burn out. There is no winning in the work, only surviving.

Nor was there anything for a detective in a man writing down an appointment with his sister in his notebook. That he would refer to her by her married surname instead of her first was worth a closer look. Maybe.

The article identified Hilda Stoudenmire Myrtle as a resident of Birmingham. When I finished my pancakes I called

Information from a pay telephone outside, got her number, and used it. The woman who answered listened to my short spiel and agreed to see me.

Birmingham started expanding after the last big war as the waiting room for Grosse Pointe, a place where new money was left to mellow and season in brick splitlevels before moving into the great Prohibition-era mausoleums on Lake Shore Drive. Then when inflation, taxes, and the servant problem began converting the mansions into museums and homes for the elderly, the new money, growing slightly used now, decided to stay in Birmingham and Bloomfield Hills, its richer bastard child. The streets are resurfaced regularly and the homes, while considerably less imposing than the glandular cases in Grosse Pointe, are beginning to look suspiciously like mansions, although their tax-shy residents are quick to deny any such assertion. Nobody wants to be called rich in a democracy.

The Myrtle home was an older ranchstyle in one of the less pretentious neighborhoods, with brick facing up to the windowsills, white aluminum siding above that, and a tricycle on the lawn, one of the new plastic jobs that no one will ever find affectionately preserved in a middle-aged citizen's garage. An impressive display of irises and poppies with big orange petals like crepe paper grew under the windows. There was a FOR SALE sign by the curb with the name of a local real estate firm printed on it. I pushed a button on the front porch and got Dvorak.

Mrs. Myrtle was small and neat like her brother, with silvering brown hair brushed straight back in an abrupt manner that said she did it mostly to keep the hair away from her face, which was oval and pointed at the bottom. The frames of her tinted glasses matched her hair and made no statement beyond that. She had on a plain gray dress with a black patent-leather belt buckled around her waist and gray shoes with low heels. Her eyes were a crisper shade of gray.

She was late thirties and could pass for early fifties. The extra years looked recent.

After we established that I wasn't there to see the house she invited me into a tidy living room done in a taste that Ma Chaney would never even suspect, let alone have: all beige and gray and vacuumed and dusted to within an inch of its life. A small cluster of family photographs on the mantel saved the place from the cool impersonality of a hotel room. Sturdy appeared in none of them.

"Are you moving out?" I asked.

"When someone meets our price." She closed and locked the front door. "The house has been on the market for six weeks."

"You can see Eight Mile Road from here. People who can afford to live in Birmingham can afford to move farther from Detroit."

"Who can afford to live in Birmingham?" Her tone wasn't bantering.

"I'm sorry about Sturdy."

"Sturdy? Oh, you mean Waldo. Yes. He was a disappointment. Did you say you were investigating his death?"

"If I'm not interrupting something more important."

"It's not your place to judge me in my house," she said quietly.

"I'm sorry about that too." I showed her the ID. "I was hired to look into the activities of a man who had business dealings with your brother. His name was Thayer."

"I never heard the name."

"Did he ever mention a man called the Colonel? Colonel Seabrook?"

"I don't recall that either, but we didn't speak very often. We weren't close. Waldo was eleven years older than I. He left home just as I was starting school. I told this to that nice Mexican detective from Iroquois Heights."

"Cuban."

"Whichever. He was very polite. I wish I could say the same for the officer he had with him."

"Did he have a crew cut and a pair of dark glasses bolted to his face?"

She looked annoyed. "If you know them, why are you here? Don't you people compare notes?"

"I'm not with the police."

"You don't look it. But then neither did the Mexican."

"You knew what your brother did for a living?"

Something more than annoyance wrinkled the smooth neatness of her face. "Don't call it that. He could have made a real living honestly. My husband offered to put in a word for him where he worked. Waldo turned him down."

He and young Thayer had that in common. "Where does your husband work?"

"Worked." She said it quickly. "He was assistant director of plant safety at Fermi Two."

"The nuclear plant? Did he retire?"

"He quit to die. The place gave him cancer. He left there two months ago."

"I'm sorry." It was the third time I'd apologized since we met.

"No, you're not, and neither are they. But they will be. I'm suing them and I don't care if it takes ten years." She looked down at the floor, then back up at me. "You'll have to forgive me. Sometimes I lose control."

"I guess it's just as well your brother didn't take the job."

"At least he died faster."

The words had no emotion at all. She was a neat woman as I said. I got away from it.

"Waldo wrote something in his notebook about an appointment with someone named Myrtle. Did he ever call you that?"

"We were on a first-name basis. Brothers and sisters usually are, no matter how seldom they see each other."

"That's what I was thinking. Might he have meant your husband?"

"I can't think why. Except for that job offer they never had anything to talk about."

"When did they discuss the job?"

"Oh, years ago." She studied me. "Do you know who killed Waldo?"

"He bought and sold stolen merchandise. You rub up against some rough hides in that line."

"That's not an answer."

"I'm pretty sure who. I'm trying to find out why. Did your husband leave any papers?"

"What kind of papers?"

"Notes. Memos. An appointment calendar. Lists of Things To Do Today. Knowing what the meeting was about would be one place to start. When a man is murdered in his bathtub, anything he did out of the ordinary toward the last goes under a bright light."

"My husband wasn't much for writing things down," she said. "Why don't you ask him in person?"

I hesitated. "I thought he was dead."

"Not dead. Dying. This way."

She led me through an arch and down a short hall to a room with shades drawn over the windows. There was a bed in the middle with someone in it and a cloying sweet smell in the overheated air, an unmistakable sickroom odor.

"This was the dining room." Her voice was barely more than a whisper. "I had the table taken out and the bed put in when he couldn't climb stairs any longer."

"Can he talk?"

"If you listen hard."

I stood in the doorway while she went in and put a hand on his shoulder. The difference in atmosphere in that room was acute, like stepping from bright sunshine into the flowered muffled silence of a funeral home.

"Tom? There's a Mr. Walker who wants to talk to you."
On her way out she touched my sleeve. "Not too long."

I went in and sat down on the hard chair next to the bed.

Mrs. Myrtle was standing in the middle of the living room
when I came back. She looked as if she'd been waiting there
all along. Her face wore a question. It was not so much pre-
maturely aged as cracked inside, like an old vase with fresh
enamel.

"Maybe something," I said. "I have to check it out."

She nodded. "I'm used to not being told anything. The
doctors are good at that."

"They're also expensive."

"Yes."

"Is that why you're selling the house?"

"Certainly not. We —"

"I just spent ten minutes with your husband. He's past
lying."

She ran her right hand up her left arm. Nodded again.
"The insurance only pays part of it. I'm not suing the plant.
We can't afford a lawyer. But the plant should pay for ev-
erything. It killed him."

"Where's your son?" Most of the pictures on the mantel
included a redheaded boy of about six.

"We — I sent him to camp. I want him to remember his
father the way he was. As it is I can hardly remember him
that way myself. And yet he's only been like this a little over
a month. So fast."

"After a while you'll remember him the way you want to."

"It's like he's dead already. You know the worst part? The
worst part is knowing I'll have to go through it all over again
when he does die."

I wanted a cigarette, but there wasn't an ashtray in the
room. "You both knew he was dying long before he quit."

"Yes. He went to the security director, the plant doctor,

the union. Nobody would help. Everyone said they were very sorry, but the illness was unrelated to his work and so he wasn't entitled to compensation. Wasn't entitled. After twelve years without a single sick day, and breathing that poison the whole time. Lying there like —" She broke. It didn't last long. When it was over she said, "I have arrangements to make for Waldo, so if you're finished."

I thanked her and left. It was warm out and the air was clean. I sucked it in in long drafts, clearing my lungs of the sweetish smell of decay, my brain of images of living skeletons as white as the sheets they lay between, speaking in short breathy bleats to strangers in darkened rooms with no son there to tell good-bye.

I sawed the Mercury's engine into life and took off with all four windows down and the fresh air rushing in.

—= 25 =—

I KNEW NOW what Sturdy had been up to and why he was
so important to the Colonel. It was crazy as a frog's hat,
but then nothing about the case had made sense from
the beginning. I might have been living in a Picasso painting
for all the way things added up.

I called the Macomb County Sheriff's Department from a
drugstore booth and asked for Galvin. While I was waiting
I broke open a fresh pack of Winstons.

"Galvin don't come on till four," said a gravel voice. "This
is Sergeant Czolgosz."

I blew smoke at the glass. "Art Winfield, Eyewitness News.
How's that man doing who was shot at Emma Chaney's
place last night?"

"They upgraded him to serious this morning. Hey, is this
on the air?"

"Tape. Has he been identified?"

"Not yet. The docs won't let us talk to him yet."

"Is Ma Chaney still in custody?"

"You kidding? She didn't even take off her coat."

"Thanks, Sergeant."

"Will this be on at six?"

I said that was up to the news director. You never know when you might need someone later.

I hung up and cracked the door to let the smoke out. A big woman in a flowered dress who had been standing near the booth earlier replaced a jar of cologne on a display and started in my direction. I pulled the door shut, got out my notebook, and called Constance Thayer at her sister's place in Redford. The big woman stumped back to the cosmetics display.

"Something?" asked Mrs. Thayer.

"Everything except Doyle Junior," I said. "Where can we meet?"

"Are you going to try to talk me into firing you again?"

"Never twice."

"Here's no good," she said. "Do you know the Blue Heron in West Bloomfield? It's a restaurant."

"Only when I'm running an expense account." I looked at my watch. "Can you make it by three?"

"I'll have to call ahead. It's a popular place."

"I guess that means I have to buy a necktie."

"What happened to the ones you had?"

"Long story. I'll see you at three."

When I came out, the big woman set down a bottle of nail polish hastily, caught it when it fell off the edge of the shelf, put it back, and charged the booth. I barely got out of her way.

The Blue Heron occupied a small building off Orchard Lake Road, built of orange brick with vines growing up the outside and young men in blue blazers stationed out front who soaked you a buck to move your car ten feet and leave it. A blonde hostess in blue taffeta and a scarlet bustier smiled at me coolly and led me to a booth in back, one of those awkward arrangements where you and your companion sat hip to hip and reacted out of the sides of your faces like cons in the exercise yard. Constance Thayer was there, looking red-haired and expensively tanned in a green satin blouse with a plunging front and a gold crescent-shaped pendant resting between her breasts. She had a black hat the size and shape of a melon wedge pinned to the side of her head, decorated with a green feather. Hats on women were coming back, and that was okay with me. It meant the end of utility hairstyles and everything that went with them, from lime-colored slacks with front zippers to colorless lipstick and men's tuxedos in women's sizes and stone-washed denims with designer patches, all the dumpy fashion paraphernalia of the unisex society.

She smiled up at me. "You bought a good one."

I ran a thumb down behind the black-and-silver rep tie I'd picked up at a men's store on the way there and sat down next to her. The gold-jacketed busboy who'd pulled the table out for me shoved it into my solar plexus. "Nice place. I think I saw Prince Philip handing out towels in the men's room."

"The owner used to be a friend. I've been here fifteen minutes and he hasn't been out to say hello."

"Did you expect him to?"

"I suppose not. I've learned a lot about friendship recently. Mainly that it isn't as common as we think. The genuine kind, anyway."

"There are friends and friends. Life's easier if you don't expect too much of them."

"Do you have any friends?" she asked.

"None, if you mean the kind you can let out your stomach with at a barbecue. If you mean the kind you can call when you're lying in an alley with a broken head, a couple." My menu came. "You ordered?"

"Yes. The stuffed breast of turkey is very good."

"So's a Cadillac."

"I'm buying."

"Wrong." I ordered coffee and a chicken salad sandwich with a Parisian accent. The waiter, a tall man no older than the car hops outside, with girlish features and large hips, carried my menu away. I slid around the semicircle until I could look at Mrs. Thayer.

"Doyle Junior's friends don't get any better with time," I said. "It was just dumb luck he lived long enough to get shot at home."

"I wish he hadn't."

"I know a deputy police chief who wishes the same thing."

"What have you found out?"

"Everything."

I shut up while the busboy tonged ice into our glasses and filled them from a bottle, turning the neck as he finished to avoid spilling any. When he left I told Mrs. Thayer everything except what I'd learned at the Myrtle house. When I was through she set fire to the cigarette she'd been holding since before I started.

"Two murders." She spat smoke. "Three, if you count Doyle. That's just the kind of thing I got out of films to avoid."

"It has a way of jumping social classes."

"I knew it was bad when you came in. You looked bleak."

"It's the tie."

"Please don't joke about it."

I shrugged. "It's bad. It will probably get worse. Things generally do."

"You didn't say what this man Sturdy had that everyone seems to want."

"I will when I can prove I'm not screwy. If I'm not, it makes Doyle's little eccentricity a dangerous obsession, and that's good for you, but I need evidence. I can buy the letter of introduction Sturdy gave Doyle to give to Ma Chaney if

I meet her price. That's a link, but it's not enough.

"The letter threw me off," I went on. "I assumed Sturdy wrote it so Ma would accept Doyle. What he really did was send Doyle to Ma so Ma could vouch for Sturdy. He had something to sell, something no other small-time fence could get his hands on. He had one buyer, but with Doyle in on the auction there was no telling how high the bidding would go."

"Dangerous."

"When you've been diving off the low board your whole life, everything about the high board looks dangerous. You have nothing to compare it to. Sturdy missed and landed on his head; not his strongest feature, or he wouldn't have gotten big eyes to begin with."

"What about the Polaris missile Doyle bought from the Chaney woman?"

"A good saleswoman will make her pitch, even if you just came in to use the bathroom. The fact that Doyle bought it shows which way his thoughts were headed."

"But you won't say which way that was."

"It's nutty," I said. "It's like being in a cartoon, and I haven't even met Daddy Warbucks yet."

"The Colonel?"

I nodded. "I've got an appointment with him tomorrow morning."

"Alone?"

"At first. Anything else would send him underground. If he comes in any way but hard, this whole thing has been just a dream. I'll wake up with my car safe in my garage with no holes in it and the usual bills to pay. Shooter and Sturdy will still be in business and I won't have shot anyone. That part's okay. You'll be someone whose face I saw on a magazine cover. I'm not sure how I feel about that part."

She rested her chin on the hand holding the cigarette. "Meaning?"

"I'd hate to miss out on a chicken salad sandwich that would keep me in groceries for two days."

Our meals came. The young man set down our dishes with a minimum of clatter, filled my cup from a miniature silver pot, and parked the pot on a blue enamel trivet shaped like a long-necked bird. He had fine white hands with slender fingers like a croupier's.

"That's not what you meant," she said when he'd withdrawn. She hadn't changed positions.

"Maybe not. I've got a rule."

"May I hear it?"

"Don't fish off the company pier."

"I have one question."

"I don't want to hear it."

She took her hand away from her chin, flicked ash into a black ceramic tray with another long-necked blue bird in the bottom, and puffed at the cigarette like Marlene Dietrich. "Where were you planning on sleeping tonight?"

=== 26 ===

THE SISTER'S HOME was a frame saltbox on Pembroke, one of a row of them with small square lawns and a basketball hoop over the door of every third garage. An ancient yellow school bus bearing the name of a Bible academy let off some of its cargo in front of the house next door and pulled away from the curb with a snort of air brakes and a drum roll of old pistons, after which I turned into the driveway. Mrs. Thayer had taken a cab to the restaurant.

"Jeanine's in Toledo overnight," she said, unlocking the front door. "She goes there sometimes to stay with my brother-in-law when he's on the road. He sells office equipment."

"Somebody has to."

There was too much furniture in the small living room, too many fragile porcelain figures on spindly racks, too many pictures on the walls. It spoke of a home that had been lived in a while and had grown around the residents. I liked it fine.

Mrs. Thayer laid her purse on a clear space of table otherwise cluttered with magazines and souvenir ashtrays. "Is it too early for a drink?"

"A drink doesn't know what time it is," I said. "Scotch, if you've got it. Anything else if you haven't."

She went out of the room and came back three minutes later with two tall glasses and handed me one. We sat down on a horsehair sofa, clinked them, and drank.

"I'm out of practice," she said. "Do I seduce you or do you seduce me?"

"At four-thirty in the afternoon?"

"A bed doesn't know what time it is."

I lit a cigarette and deposited the match on Paul Revere's face, compliments of Greenfield Village. "The papers said your son was home the night you shot Doyle. Is he going to testify?"

"No." She turned her glass around in her hands. "I haven't even told Leslie what school I put him in. He'll never be able to forget if people keep bringing it up around him."

"The prosecution will subpoena him if the defense doesn't. Don't think they won't be able to find him."

"He didn't see anything."

"What didn't he see, the shooting or the beating earlier?"

"Neither. He was in bed."

"I used to sneak out of bed to watch *The Untouchables*," I said. "My parents never knew it."

"He didn't see anything."

"He must have heard something. You can't slap a woman around without making some kind of noise. It would be another penny on your side of the scale."

"No." She drank.

"You're lucky you got Dorrance. A lawyer without a book contract would've dropped you long ago."

"What about a private detective without one?"

"Lawyers are smarter." I drained my glass and set it down. "It's been a long day. Tomorrow's going to be longer. If I can borrow this sofa and a blanket."

"You can sleep in the guest room. I'll use the bedroom. Look, I'm not in the habit of shooting all the men I sleep with."

"You're not in the habit of sleeping with all the men you meet either. All this publicity about the films you made is getting to you. You don't have to be what they say you are just because they say it."

"Is that what you think I'm doing?"

"Everyone does it."

"You don't."

"I'm a detective. I just reflect light." I got up. "Thanks for the bed. I'm moteled out."

"Thanks for dinner."

"Forget it. I've got a rich client."

She went into the guest room ahead of me and removed some of her things. Afterward it still smelled of her. I had another smoke by the window, thinking of exactly nothing, then undressed and hung up my clothes and stretched out between the sheets. I didn't draw the curtains. An artificially darkened room would have reminded me too much of the one where Hilda Myrtle's husband lay, waiting.

I was waiting too.

For a time I watched the spackled ceiling. Then I turned onto my left side and stared at the door. That was too obvious, so I rolled over and looked at the window. A maple branch hung low outside, heavy with leaves. The sun threw their gray shadows in a mottled pattern on the floor, and when the breeze stirred them the shadows shimmered like light on water. Someone next door was dribbling a basketball unevenly on asphalt, the hollow impacts punctuated at irregular intervals by the flap and twang of the ball going through a hoop. Elsewhere a screen door banged shut. A helicopter wobbled overhead on its way to monitor the evening traffic back from the beaches.

Somewhere in there, waiting, I fell asleep. I woke up in the dark, turned on the bedside lamp, and checked my watch. Just past nine. The door was still closed. I sat up for a while smoking, then put out the butt and switched off the lamp and settled back down.

She came in a few minutes later and climbed in next to me. The warmth of her body filled the space under the covers. She was all heated flesh and cool silk and sinewy arms and legs and lips searching. This time I helped her.

=== 27 ===

SHE JOINED ME in the living room shortly after sunrise. I was sitting on the sofa cleaning the Beretta from a cheap kit I'd bought during my visit to Meijer's and put in the car. She had on a blue chiffon robe and the sunlight through the window made a halo of her hair, still damp from the shower. The smell of scented soap mingled with the sharp gun-oil odor.

"Do you think you'll need that?"

"I'll try not to."

"Isn't it awfully early?"

"I like to get there first." I wiped off each of the cartridges and reloaded the clip. There was nothing wrong with the way Shooter had loaded it, but if there had been, there were much worse times to find that out.

"Can't you send the police in your place?"

"Colonel Seabrook will just shake hands all around and go back to the wars. They've got nothing on him."

"And you do."

I rammed the clip home and chambered a shell. "Not yet."

"You're going to make him confess by shoving a gun at him?"

"Guns don't work that way except on television." I stood, seated the automatic under my belt behind my right hip, and put on my jacket.

She crossed to the table that was holding up the magazines and ashtrays and took something out of a drawer. "In case you run out of bullets."

I took it. It was a nickel-plated Browning .25 automatic with a mother-of-pearl handle, shiny all over and full of sin. When I made a fist it disappeared. "Yours or your sister's?"

"Doyle gave it to me for our first anniversary. I was afraid to have it around when Jack was small, so I gave it to Jeanine. Even when Doyle started his collection I made him promise never to leave anything lying around loaded."

I sprang the clip one-handed and thumbed it back in. "This one's loaded."

"Jeanine. She's alone here most of the time. I don't even know how."

"I'll try to get it back to you." I put it in my side pocket.

"Don't bother. I've had my fill of them." She laughed shortly. "I wish I knew how to cook breakfast. I don't feel right sending you off on an empty stomach."

I stood in front of her. "You don't need to know how to cook."

"Are you sorry?"

"I think I'm supposed to ask you that."

"I'm not. It was the only way I felt safe with Doyle when he was — that way. I'd forgotten what it was like when it's for pleasure."

"I don't know how you stood him so long."

"Even a beaten dog likes to eat."

"The hell with that. You were on your own before."

"Jack wasn't."

"Kids are tough. They fight back."

"So do wives. Some wives."

I took a card from my wallet and held it out. After a moment she accepted it. "Horace Livingood," she read. "Who's he?"

"Treasury agent. He represented ATF on the weapons sweep in your husband's basement. Call him after I leave. Tell him to meet me at my office at eight-thirty."

"How many cops does that make?"

"Three, with Alderdyce and Romero, not counting infantry support. They can work out jurisdictions among themselves. Better tell him about the others. The paperwork's murder when badges shoot badges."

"You think there'll be shooting?"

"It was just an expression."

"That's not an answer."

"When there's shooting, it means somebody made a mistake. If I work it right there won't be."

She turned away. "They ought to throw all the guns in the Detroit River. Sporting rifles on up."

"Throw the knives in after them," I said. "Don't forget the garrotes and saps and all the bottles with skulls and crossbones on the labels. Then they'll just beat each other to death with rocks. It's not the guns you have to take out. It's the shooters."

"Like me."

I said, "You never shot anyone."

It took a moment; or maybe it sank in right away and she used the moment to rearrange her face. When she turned around it looked confused. "What did that mean?"

"Doyle Junior was shot with an automatic. The loading principle is the same as this one." I patted the .25 in my coat pocket. "You just told me you don't know the first thing about how to load it."

"It was loaded already."

"You said you made him promise never to leave one lying around loaded."

"He broke it. Do you think a promise meant anything to him when he was in that condition?"

"The level of drugs and alcohol the coroner found in his system would've kept him from putting together a coherent sentence, much less loading a gun. If he got that tanked up whenever he beat you he couldn't have done it, and when he wasn't he wouldn't have. You told me yourself what a dear he was when he was straight."

"Don't, Amos."

"Weapons were his hobby. Fathers like to share their interests with their sons. Doyle would've shown Jack how to care for a gun. How to use it. How to load it."

"No. I shot him."

"It was a big house, but not so big young Jack wouldn't hear his father beating up on his mother. The last time was one time too many. After it was over, when you were lying somewhere recovering and Doyle had passed out naked on the bed, Jack sneaked downstairs. He probably selected a gun he'd handled before under his father's supervision. He loaded it and went back upstairs and used it."

She slapped me. The crack made my ears ring, but I didn't move. "You're not doing him any favors by standing the rap," I said. "A thing like that is a time bomb. He'll wind up making some psychiatrist rich."

"It's a lie."

"You're a lie. Constance Thayer, the notorious spouse-killer of Iroquois Heights. That's the lie. The joke is how many people were willing to help you tell it."

She raised her hand again. This time I caught it. I said, "One's all you get for free. After that I slap back."

"Go ahead. I'm used to it."

I forced down her hand, kept hold of it, and grasped the other. "Tell Dorrance the truth. He'll know what to do. If he's still part man and not all lawyer he'll introduce the truth, put Jack on the stand, and get this thing out before it starts to fester. Nobody's going to put him in reform school. He'll get help."

"It happened the way I said it happened."

"A mother protects her child, right?"

"Something like that."

"Not the other way around."

She said nothing.

"That's just a role." I released her then. She drew back. The look was back, only different; hunted. It was like that scene in *Dracula* where the woman is exposed as a vampire and her expression changes from seductive to feral. I laughed then. It sounded hollow even to me.

"You enjoy playing it, don't you? You're not thinking of Jack at all. It's just another acting job, only this time you get to keep your clothes on."

"You're fired. Get out of my sister's house."

"Lady, I quit."

"Amos."

I paused with my hand on the doorknob. I didn't feel the least bit like Rhett Butler.

"It isn't just a role. My son is all I have."

I left.

It was a high hot day, crisp, without humidity. The sky went straight up for a thousand miles, a long blue tube with the earth at the bottom and scattered clouds stuck at the top. The air was dizzyingly clear. I breathed in a double lungful. Freedom. I owed nothing to anybody. I could go anywhere in the world from that spot, Singapore or Flint. I could play miniature golf around the corner or fish for marlin in the Gulf Stream. There was no fine print on any contract saying I had to go to the office and meet Colonel Winston Seabrook.

I cranked up the Mercury and took off in that direction. I'm a lousy miniature golfer anyway.

*

Guns.

The history of guns is the history of Detroit, from the day Cadillac's men dazzled the local Indians with the rattle and flame of their muskets to last Friday, when a sixteen-year-old boy shot down another boy at the downtown Taco Bell for looking at him wrong. Chief Pontiac tried to seize Fort Detroit by smuggling sawed-off muzzle-loaders through the gate under his braves' blankets, and Harry Bennett mounted Lewis machine guns atop the Ford factory to mow down picketing auto workers. John Brown, while visiting the Detroit end of the Underground Railroad, had bought the guns for his botched raid on Harpers Ferry. Detroit built the gunboats and bombers that did more to win the Second World War than Churchill's cigar, and it was automatic gunfire in the darkened alleys of Twelfth Street that made a waking nightmare of the 1967 race riots. The battering of Thompsons along the Detroit River had helped to make the twenties roar. Pretty little pearl-handled ladies' automatics, big black businesslike Frontier Colts, cheap greasy Saturday Night Thumpers as dangerous to their handlers as to their intended targets, nasty plastic-and-sheet-metal burp guns with foreign names stamped on the barrels, stately Lugers, squat-nosed Police Specials, silenced .22's, amplified .45's, sawed-off shotguns, sniper rifles with scopes, pocket derringers, two-man bazookas, Mausers, Marlins, Mannlichers, Remingtons and Rugers, Springfields and Smith & Wessons, Winchesters and Webleys, Berettas and Brownings, Hawkens, Henries, Hotchkisses, and howitzers — any one of them held as strong a claim to the city as Ty Cobb and the Model T. Question: What's Detroit without guns? Answer: Cleveland. Joke.

And now the biggest gun of them all, bigger than all the rest put together, was loaded and cocked and ready to fire. All it needed was someone dumb enough to try to stand in front of it.

AMOS WALKER

The letters, white plastic on the black background of the directory in the foyer of my building, were new, the first improvement that had been made there since plumbing. At the moment mine was the only name on the third floor. The baby photographer next door had been hauled downtown for pederasty, the travel agent had been locked out for nonpayment of rent, one business had failed, another had outgrown the place and moved uptown, and the office at the end of the hall where mail was delivered daily and picked up on Wednesdays by nobody knew who had never had a name. The stairs made melancholy noises when I climbed them.

Half empty as it was, the building felt lonelier than the usual early Monday morning, like a dying cell in a terminal body; but that was the mood I was in. It was just the Lysol in the hallway outside my reception room that made it smell like a mortician's workshop, only the humming of the building super's vacuum cleaner in an empty downstairs office that sounded like the incinerator in a crematorium. The tinkle of my keys was ridiculously loud as I shook loose the one to the door.

A shaft of metal, Arctic cold, touched the tender bone behind my right ear, sending a dull thrum of remembered pain throughout my skull. At the same time a hand reached under my jacket and pulled the Beretta out from under my belt.

"Don't it pay to get up with the birds, though?" twanged Hubert Darling's voice close behind me. "Let's go, slugger. The Colonel ain't got all day."

28

HE FOLLOWED ME downstairs and out the door, where a dark blue Chrysler sedan was parked illegally in front of the building. I had seen it twice before. His gun prodded my lower back. "Inside, champ."

I got in. A man was sitting in the back seat on the right side. He was bigger and uglier than Hubert, with a nose-heavy face curdled with acne and a prison haircut that went with his gray pallor. He had on a blue Windbreaker over a mesh T-shirt that needed washing. It had been years, but I recognized him.

"Hello, Jerry," I said. "Your brother told me you were still in Jackson."

After a second he showed me a set of long amber teeth like a horse's. "Work-release program. I missed the last bus."

"Was that before or after you and Hubert sapped me down at the fairgrounds?"

"I didn't *think* you was out the whole time."

Hubert opened the driver's door and slid under the wheel. Jerry turned the flat blue Darling eyes on him. "You frisk him?"

"Got this here." He held up the Beretta.

"You *frisk* him?"

"Didn't have to. It stuck out like —"

Jerry cuffed the back of Hubert's head. "Shithead. On your knees facing me, Walker. Hube, cover him."

As I turned around I took the little Browning out of my side pocket and stuffed it down between the seat cushions. My body was between it and Hubert. I knelt on the seat with my back to the windshield and my hands on the headrest. Jerry leaned forward, patted all my pockets, and felt me under the arms and between my thighs. He didn't overlook my ankles. Finally he sat back. "Okay, Hube."

When I was facing the other way Hubert stuck a pair of black plastic wraparound sunglasses at me. I put them on. Someone had taped aluminum foil over the inside of the lenses, blocking out all light. Hubert buckled the seat belt across my arms. "For your own good, slugger," he said. "If you forget and take 'em off, we get to kill you."

Jerry said, "Shut up and drive."

The engine started smoothly and we began moving. For a while I tried to keep track of the turns, but Hubert should have made his living flashing baseball signals; after we circled two blocks I stopped counting. Listening was no good either, because he had the radio tuned in hard to a hillbilly station. Well, I knew from the TV set in Sturdy's room that he liked things loud.

It seemed we drove for hours; at least eighteen killings, twenty-two infidelities, eleven honky-tonks, and nine incarcerations, Grand Ole Opry Time. It was probably closer to forty-five minutes. When the pavement smoothed out under the tires I knew we had left the surface streets for an expressway, which in the immediate area narrowed the options to seven. I knew too when we left asphalt for gravel. That continued for a long time, and then we turned onto something more private, by the neglected feel of loose stones and sharp ruts registered in my stomach and fillings. Shortly after that we rolled to a stop.

Someone opened my door and undid the seat belt. I stumbled getting out, put my hand between the cushions, grasped the little automatic, and returned it to my side pocket, hiding the maneuver with my body. I was walking on grass. A moist smell of fresh manure reached me. I had a pretty good idea then where I was.

We went inside, through some rooms, and down a flight of thickly carpeted stairs. I was fairly sure, although nobody opened his mouth, that others had joined us. The air was more crowded and I smelled a new brand of after-shave. At length we stopped. A door closed behind us.

"Well, take them off."

This was a different voice, but slightly familiar. Someone removed the sunglasses before I could lift a hand and I blinked in the light. It was indirect, illuminating walls paneled in squares of walnut with the grains set at right angles and a wall-to-wall shag carpet with orange and brown fibers. There were some chairs made of steel tubing and molded plastic and a grandfather clock that had been knocking out the minutes for about eighty years; but however you decorate a basement you're still underground. I had a Darling on either side and there were three other men in the room. Two were dressed in black trousers and navy turtlenecks, lightweight but still too warm for the season, with the trousers tucked into mirror-finish black combat boots. Their faces were unlined and almost identical, the way they always are when their owners haven't been around much past twenty years and a military barber has been at them. They wore olive-drab berets at the same precise angle and held M-16 assault rifles across their torsos in sentry position.

The third man stood between them facing me with his feet spread and his hands behind his back. He had been cut from the same bolt, but a lot earlier. He was six feet four in a tan suit tailored military fashion, with patch pockets and shiny black buttons and a knitted black tie on a khaki shirt. His thinning hair was black except for snowy puffs over his ears and combed diagonally across his long skull. He wore glasses with thick black rims whose lenses reflected the light in flat circles, with all the magnifying properties of clear windowpanes; they were just a gimmick to cover the wrinkles around his eyes. He looked fifty.

The door opened behind me. I turned my head and looked at another young man dressed like the others, who closed the door and stood in front of it with his M-16 across his chest.

I turned back. "I'm more dangerous than I thought."

The man in the tan suit looked at the Darlings. "You searched him for weapons?"

"Yeah." Hubert stepped forward, took the Beretta out of his waistband, and handed it to him butt-first.

The man in the tan suit kicked out the clip and pocketed it, then ran back the slide. The cartridge in the chamber popped out and landed noiselessly on the carpet. Without pausing he swept the barrel across Hubert's face. The steel sight split his left cheek like a ripe orange. He yelped and staggered back two steps. His brother started forward, then stopped.

" 'Yes, sir' is the response," said the man in the tan suit.

Jerry said, "We ain't in your fucking army."

The man in the tan suit moved his head slightly. There was a slight rustle from behind, then a sickening thump at my side, and Jerry fell in a crumple. The young man from the door stood over him holding his assault rifle with the butt forward.

"Let me hear you say it," the man in the tan suit told Hubert.

"Yes, sir." He was holding a bloody handkerchief to his cheek and looking at his unconscious brother.

Colonel Seabrook — it had to be him, even aside from the deceptively youthful voice I had heard over the telephone — admired the Beretta. "An excellent pistol, although I prefer the old forty-five for aesthetic reasons. But you can't fight the next war with weapons from the last. You were in Vietnam, weren't you, Walker?"

"Yes, sir."

"You don't have to say that. As a matter of fact I wish you wouldn't. You have a way of saying it I don't like."

"I didn't like it much myself."

"I was there too, of course. Lieutenant, First Battalion, Ninth Marines. We used to shoot tigers outside Quang Tri when things got slow. It was better sport than hunting Charlie. When a tiger starts eating villagers it means he's too old to chase other game, but he's smarter than the usual run because in a country crawling with armed men a tiger doesn't grow old by being dumb; too smart anyway to go after a tethered goat. We used villagers."

"Get many?"

"I sent home a dozen rugs."

"I meant villagers."

Jerry Darling, coming to, groaned. Seabrook ignored him. "You know what it was like. They didn't care who won as long as the rice paddy wasn't spoiled, and they'd help out either side if it meant the war would go down the road. It's the same here. The true soldier fights for the fight's sake. Certainly not for president or country, both of whom would rather he died over there once the thing's done. As soon as they stop needing it they can't take the machine apart fast enough."

"Nice speech. I bet your cub scouts eat it up."

"I trained these men myself. I didn't have much to work with in the beginning. The current generation is only interested in making a lot of money so they can afford toys. I'd almost rather have those sniveling pups who set fire to flags twenty years ago; at least they had spirit. But I'm happy with the way these men turned out."

"They're as slick a band of burglars as I ever met," I said.

"They're soldiers. You of all people should recognize the breed."

"I'm not a soldier."

"Of course you are." He held up the Beretta. "Anyone who straps on a gun for someone else who can't or won't is a soldier. The uniform is optional."

"Is that why you Pearl-Harbored my car in the warehouse district?"

"That was a mistake. Separating the allies from the enemy isn't as easy as it used to be."

"Sturdy and the Shooter would agree."

"Minor casualties."

"You're short a man," I said. "He's probably talking to the cops right now. I didn't quite let all the blood out of him at Ma Chaney's place."

"He won't say anything."

I knew then that he wouldn't, ever, even if he recovered and outlived his sentence. I changed tactics. There were too many automatic weapons in the room to give much thought to the tiny pistol in my pocket.

"You're too tidy for your own good, Colonel. All I wanted in the beginning was a line on Doyle Thayer Junior's activities in the gun trade, enough to convince a jury that his wife wasn't doing society any great harm in killing him. If you hadn't tried to ambush me I'd never have suspected you were involved in the home invasions or the other thing. You compounded the error by trying to take out Ma Chaney. She talks when she's mad. Maybe she never sat in on any of your training sessions."

"Who'd listen to a crazy old bat who's also a known felon?"

"Nobody, until you made her worth listening to. Attempted murder is a great credibility builder." I let him

186

chew on it. "I won't lecture you about Shooter. Doing him with my gun at the fairgrounds was somebody's half-baked idea of getting in good with you. I guess you thought a show of loyalty would make the Colonel forget how quickly you ditched Ma for him, right, Hube?"

Hubert, still holding the handkerchief to his face, said, "Keep it up, champ. I ain't forgot I still owe you one for the other day."

"Even a big chief can't know what all the Indians are up to all the time," I told Seabrook. "But it wouldn't have happened if your highly trained Hitler Youth had shot me instead of my car."

"Water over the dam. I never waste time refighting old battles." He stroked the Beretta. "I'm sorry I couldn't meet you at your office. You hung up before I had a chance to explain that I always choose my own rendezvous sites."

"You picked a good one. Who'd have predicted Mark Proust's basement? Especially with elections coming up."

Jerry had pried himself into a cross-legged position on the floor with his head in his hands. The man who had hit him had returned to his station at the door. Jerry's labored breathing was the loudest thing in the room for a long moment.

Seabrook glared at Hubert. "I gave orders to blindfold him as soon as he was in the car."

"We did. He didn't see nothing the whole way." He sounded afraid, which was a surprise. I hadn't thought he was that smart.

"You should have covered my nose too," I said. "I was here once before, although not in the basement. I'm not Elizabeth Taylor, but I know a horse farm when I smell one."

The Colonel shook his head sadly. "I take back what I said before. You wouldn't make a good soldier. You think too much."

"It's a fault. Sometimes I envy Hubert and Jerry."

"They don't think enough. But they're useful, up to a point." As he spoke, the Colonel removed the Beretta's clip from his pocket, rammed it into the handle, and racked a cartridge into the chamber. He thumbed off the safety and shot Hubert Darling. The bullet pierced the bridge of his nose and took off the back of his head.

Hubert took a month to fall. His head came up as if someone had called his name. That pulled his split cheek away from the handkerchief in his hand, and in the instant of consciousness left to him he started to raise it to the cut. It never got there, because by then his knees were bending and he turned and sort of screwed himself down until his center of gravity changed and he fell the rest of the way with a flop. After that he lay as motionless as a sack of mud.

Jerry groaned. It was hard to tell if it was because of his brother or his own aching head.

"I should have done that when he executed Shooter against my orders," said the Colonel, absently wiping the gun up and down one leg of his trousers. His voice sounded muffled in the echo of the blast. "I definitely should have done it after Stoudenmire. But I rather like the justice of it this way: He used Walker's gun on Shooter, I use Walker's gun on him."

I thought of telling him it wasn't my gun, but decided he wouldn't appreciate it. What I did say sounded a lot like nothing. The air smelled of brimstone.

29

SOMEONE BATTERED at the door. The noise was loud in the throbbing silence following the shot and Colonel Seabrook's words. The Colonel's eyes flicked over my shoulder to the man at the door. He nodded. The door was opened.

"What was that shot?" Proust barreled in past me, glanced down at Jerry Darling being sick on the rug, saw his brother lying on his face with the back of his head gone. He recoiled. "I said no killing. What did you do to me?"

"It doesn't matter," Seabrook said. "I told you the blindfold wouldn't work. Walker guessed where he is."

Proust looked at me, or rather through me. He was wearing a short-sleeved plaid sport shirt and tight jeans that emphasized his paunch. His face was grayer than usual. "I didn't want him here in the first place. You should've taken him somewhere else."

"You should've sent me packing when I proposed our partnership. But you didn't, and I did, and that's the big picture. A good commander doesn't waste time wishing things were better. It's beginning to smell in here." He strode toward the door, avoiding the gore underfoot.

"What about him?" Proust was looking again at Jerry, who wasn't looking at anything but what he'd had for breakfast.

"A man should be with his brother." On his way out, Seabrook glanced at the man at the door.

The other two sentries came away from the wall. I turned and followed the Colonel out. Proust stumbled along at the rear. Behind us the third sentry's M-16 burped briefly, like an engine starting and stalling. He came out a moment later, drawing the door shut. Blue smoke curled out with him.

We were in a larger room, paneled similarly, with a ceramic tile floor speckled like blue cheese and a furnace and a pool table in opposite corners. Rectangular windows along the ceiling let in light between blades of grass growing outside. The Colonel stood at the far end of the pool table with the first two sentries behind him, resting his hands on the corners of the table. He looked a little like Eisenhower studying a map of Normandy.

"Cut to the chase," he told me. "Have you got it?"

"Would I be here if I didn't?"

"You might, if my reconnaissance reports on you are reliable. You're what we jarheads used to call a nighthawker. You go it alone and fight by your own rules. That's fine when the nighthawker's in command; he wins battles and seizes objectives no one dared count on back at HQ. When he isn't, more often than not he gets shot for insubordination, if he comes back at all. Individual heroism's good for the folks back home. It helps recruitment. On the front it just spoils the casualty projections."

"I'm not a hero," I said. "Just curious. What do you want it for?"

"Why should I tell you?"

"Call it a last request."

"Are you planning on dying soon?"

I leaned on the other end of the pool table, imitating his pose. The little automatic shifted in my pocket. "You as much as told Proust just now I wouldn't leave here alive," I said. "The blindfold didn't work, and anyway it was just a gesture to keep him from squawking too loud about using his house. What's it matter whether I die before or after I hand over the stuff? I just don't want to die ignorant."

"You're safe at least until I have the fissionable material. After that you're on your own. But then you always were."

"Fissionable material."

His face twitched. It was as near as he would come to smiling when he wasn't rereading Clausewitz. "Plutonium. Do you mean to say you have it in your possession and you aren't even aware of the terminology?"

"Give some people a gun and they'll shoot you with it. They don't have to know how it was made. What are you planning to blow up?"

"That's my secret."

"So's the place where I stashed the plutonium."

"Do you think I can't get that out of you?"

"You could have gotten it out of Sturdy the same way, but he took precautions, or told you he did. I imagine they took the form of a sealed envelope left with someone to be mailed to the cops in case of his death. It's an old tune but it still holds up."

"I don't hear sirens."

"The mail's always slow on Monday. You could start hauling on my toenails, but that takes time. You were working against a deadline from the start or you wouldn't have scheduled those home invasions so close together. You needed money fast to buy the plutonium from Sturdy. Sturdy's been dead twenty-four hours and you still don't have the stuff. Meanwhile, what amounts to a deathbed testimony by the man Hubert accidentally killed is on its way to someone who will listen. If time were gasoline you couldn't get out of the garage."

He straightened and locked his hands behind his back. He'd made a decision.

"There is a mountain in Zimbabwe," he said. "The natives who have been to it come away with clay on their sandals. Diamond clay. So far no one knows about it beyond a dozen half-wild tribesmen and a handful of government officials, all of them in my pay. By Christmas the whole world will have heard about it, by which time I intend to be in control of the country."

"A nuclear bomb is fairly heavy as mining equipment goes. Why not use picks and shovels?"

"It won't be detonated anywhere near the mountain. A simple demonstration in the Kalahari Desert should be enough to convince the government of my ability to blow the whole place into the South Atlantic if the mountain isn't deeded to me along with all mineral rights."

"Jesus." Proust had collapsed into an overstuffed chair whose upholstery was too worn for upstairs and was mopping his face with a lawn handkerchief. The gesture reminded me of Hubert Darling. "You told me you were raising money to buy arms to sell to African revolutionaries."

"If I'd told you the truth you'd never have given me the safe harbor I needed in Iroquois Heights. You small-town crooks never think big enough. With that mountain's resources at my command, in five years I can control two thirds of the continent of Africa; in ten years, the Persian Gulf. I'll own four fifths of the world's oil. And all thanks to a string of forgotten domestic robberies in and around Detroit."

He didn't foam at the mouth or throw himself down on all fours and start gnawing at the legs of the pool table. His

voice retained its light youthful quality and his eyes were
dead gray behind the prop glasses. Well, I hadn't expected
histrionics. They aren't all like Hitler or the Ayatollah, except in the ways that count.

I said, "You've got the bomb?"

"Missile, to be precise. I have four Jupiters, outmoded but
still quite effective. The technology is a matter of public record. All I need is the juice."

"Who told Sturdy you needed it?"

"He came to me. Everyone around here knows there is
only one person to go to with a cargo like that."

"You're underestimating him," I said. "People did. He
smelled something on the wind or he wouldn't have started
working on his brother-in-law to steal the stuff from Fermi
Two. That kind of heist is never easy, but not as difficult
when you're with plant security. Myrtle didn't figure he
owed anything to the place he thought gave him cancer, so
he agreed to try."

"Try."

That was a mistake. What I said next was another, but I
was talking to keep him from thinking. "How much was
Sturdy soaking you?"

"You were his partner; you should know. Or were you?"
He took his hands from behind his back. One of them held
the Beretta. He had stuck it inside his belt under his tan
coat. "I was right about you being a nighthawker. I should
have quoted you their depressing survival statistics."

I straightened and let my hands drop from the table. The
first knuckle of my right thumb grazed the .25 in my pocket.
I might have left it with Constance Thayer for all the good
it was doing me there. I kept talking.

"Sturdy moving up into the big time was like a kid getting
his first taste of whiskey; he liked the lightheaded feeling
and wanted more. Jacking you up for all you could spare
and could score from the home invasions wasn't enough. He

went to Doyle Thayer Junior, who had the collectors' bug and the wherewithal to outbid you into next year, or for as long as he could get away with forging his father's signature on checks. That was when one of your wind-up soldiers gossiped to Ma Chaney that Sturdy wouldn't be around much longer.

"He was wrong. They didn't call him Sturdy for nothing. He'd still be with us if his heart hadn't given out while Hubert was trying to drown the truth out of him. I'll take part of that," I added. "If I hadn't forced your hand by telling you I was his partner you wouldn't have sicced Hubert on him to begin with. I thought he was safe in jail."

Seabrook wasn't listening. "You said Stoudenmire's brother-in-law agreed to try to steal the plutonium. He didn't get it, did he?"

Casually — I felt as jerky as an actor crossing a stage for the first time — I put my hands in the pockets of my jacket. The maneuver had all the unstudied naturalness of a feather dancer performing in a high wind.

"No," I said. "He got too sick and had to leave the job before he got near the stuff. Sturdy was bluffing you right along. Me too."

Tension came into that room like another person. The three sentries, spaced out expertly with identical fields of fire, gripped their automatic rifles so tightly they creaked. The Beretta in the Colonel's hand lay as steady as a stone.

We were all in our places, all the lines had been spoken. It only remained for one of us to start the show.

Jerry Darling stole it. The door to the other room bumped open, so quickly he lost his balance and fell on his side. He was a mess. His head was bleeding where the butt of an M-16 had cracked it open and the blood had trickled down his neck in a forked pattern, where it vanished inside the neck of his mesh T-shirt and mingled with more blood from a tight ragged line of bullet wounds in his chest. From there it had drenched his right sleeve and hand. The revolver in it must have been slippery. It went off when he hit the floor, squirting fire and a slug that struck the furnace with a clang and a rumble, as of a theater prop man shaking a sheet of tin to simulate thunder.

Then the thunder was silenced by a louder peal of three M-16s clearing their throats in unison. Their actions rattled and their spent shells plink-plunked to the floor and smoke smudged the room's details and Jerry's big body jerked and twitched as if attached to three strings, his mouth falling open and his eyes rolling white.

The Colonel, who had not stopped watching me since we had entered the room, was momentarily distracted. I took the small pistol out of my pocket — .25s are barely effective at best, and when fired through fabric are useless — but even as I squeezed the trigger I knew I wasn't fast enough. He was already firing the Beretta in my direction.

I thought.

I was too caught up in the moment to know that an army had come clattering down the stairs behind me, led by a coarse-featured black Detroit police inspector named Alderdyce and a delicately built Hispanic Iroquois Heights lieutenant named Romero and backed up by a dumpy Wallace Beery type of a federal agent who answered to Horace Livingood. The Beretta's bullet flicked my left jacket sleeve and splintered the staircase railing an inch to the right of Romero's right ear as he crouched and returned fire with his bone-handled service pistol. I was firing at the same time, squeezing off three rounds as fast as my trigger finger could flex and relax. The tiny automatic might have belonged to Marcel Marceau for all the noise it made in that pounding room. Four bullets, one large, three no bigger than pencil erasers, made black holes in Colonel Seabrook's tan suit. He took two steps back, then one forward, and sprawled face down across the pool table, one hand still clutching the Ber-

etta. The nails of his other hand made five distinct tracks in
the green felt as he slid to his knees. After that there was no
more room to fall and he knelt there between the wall and
the table — dreaming, no doubt, in whatever time was left
for dreaming, of conquest and diamonds.

The two local cops had brought reinforcements, and between their handguns and sawed-off shotguns they tore
apart the three young men with assault rifles like teddy
bears in a shooting gallery. It seemed the Colonel hadn't
trained them to meet armed resistance in close quarters, because later two uniformed officers were treated for minor
wounds and a third for a shattered wrist, while one of the
mercenaries was pronounced dead at the scene and another
died on the operating table at Detroit Receiving. The last
was admitted there in critical condition and upon improving
was transferred to the infirmary at the Detroit House of
Corrections.

The walnut paneling would never be the same, along with
every eardrum on the premises.

When the shooting stopped, someone had to ram a shotgun butt through two of the windows to let the smoke out.
In the clearing air, a Detroit uniform pried a white and
quivering Mark Proust's fingers loose from the back of the
overstuffed chair, behind which he had taken cover. When
he let go the chair listed toward one corner where a leg had
been shot away. A spring tore loose from the riddled fabric.

"*Caramba*," said Romero, standing among the flung and
spraddled bodies. "For this I could have stayed in Havana."

30

THE LIVING ROOM of Ernest Krell's home, large and sunken and lighted through amber panels instead of windows, looked dim and remote, like an Egyptian tomb that had remained unchanged throughout the rise and fall of the Roman Empire, the life of Christ, the Middle Ages, two world wars, and the entire career of Mason Reese. The walls were still burled walnut and I didn't much care for them because they reminded me of the paneling in Mark Proust's basement. Krell's Korean War portrait hung above it all, a proud flag on a ship in drydock.

Leslie Dorrance sat on the chalk-colored sofa reading my typewritten report. His horse face looked comforting, like a homely aunt's when you've had enough of city lights and bottled blondes. His legs were crossed in expensive brown pinstriped trousers ending in ribbed socks and the inevitable thick-soled loafers with tassels. Krell stood at the mantel in another of his black suits, this one with orange stripes to match his sunset-colored tie, clasped with the bit of shrapnel. The sharp creases in his face made it look as if it had been assembled from squares of pale metal. He never sat. I decided either his old hip wound made sitting uncomfortable or he liked people to compare him to the figure in the painting.

Constance Thayer was seated across from me with her legs crossed in a chair that matched the sofa. She had on a lightweight green summer dress and white pumps and her hair appeared rich brown in that light. She looked as if she'd gotten a good night's sleep. Well, so had I: fourteen hours, after spending all of Monday and a big slice of Monday night with cops. Today was Wednesday.

Dorrance read the last page, flipped back a couple and reread something, then closed the report. His eyes were bright. "This can all be substantiated?"

I nodded. "The cops have a deathbed testimony from the young man who died at Receiving, and the man I shot at Ma Chaney's has agreed to turn state's evidence to help truss up Proust and the other Iroquois Heights officials involved. With the Colonel dead there's no one left to be loyal to."

"Of course I don't approve," Dorrance said. "Many other lawyers would have quit the case when they found out their client had hired an investigator behind their backs a second time. However, for the first time in my life I wish we had a shorter court date. I'd like to try this before a jury while the news reports are still fresh in their minds."

"They'll be fresh enough. The nuke angle scares a lot of people. As indirectly as Doyle Junior was involved in this mess, the fact that he was interested in obtaining plutonium to arm his pet Polaris missile has got to make whoever shot him look great by comparison." I was looking at Constance as I spoke. She was busy lighting a cigarette.

Krell cleared his throat. The noise reminded me of an M-16. He rested a hand inside his coat, and *that* reminded me of an M-16. My ears were still ringing. "I knew Seabrook socially," he said. "Old soldiers, you know. He always seemed quite rational. I can't believe he had any faith in his scheme."

I moved a shoulder. "People are unhinged on the subject of nuclear arms, like I said. He was like a kid who watches television and thinks you can make anyone do whatever you want just by waving a gun at him. It's never an either/or proposition when it comes to blackmailing governments. Something would have come along. That's what the people who worry about the ozone and the population problem and the atomic bomb never understand. Something always comes along."

"Like you," said Dorrance.

"Something else if not me. There's a natural balance to these things."

The lawyer rolled the report in his hands absently. "Do you think the Chaney woman would testify that Thayer came to her to buy the Polaris? That connection needs shoring up."

"If you meet her price."

"I'm sure I can swing immunity."

"She's got that now. Macomb County's case against her fell apart when her people spirited all those weapons and explosives out of the farmhouse right under the sheriff's nose."

"Will *you* testify?"

"No." This time Constance and I were looking at each other. Her face gave up nothing.

"We need you," Dorrance said.

"It'd be just hearsay. I'll sign an affidavit if you want but I won't go to court."

"Why not?"

"Let it go, Leslie," said Constance. "Mr. Walker's made up his mind."

"Well, I wish I knew what was going on."

"If you did you wouldn't," I said.

I wanted to leave then, but Mrs. Krell came in with a tray of lemon cookies and set it on the coffee table. For once I wasn't hungry enough to eat one. They reminded me of M-16s.

After she went out, Krell said, "I think I'd better absent myself as well. I hope to work with Thayer Industries in the future and I want to avoid any suggestion of conflict."

I said, "The old man got to you, didn't he?"

He colored. "I have an organization to support. I can't drift from one client to the next like you."

"Don't explain. I sold out more cheaply than you did." I stood. "Good luck in court, Mr. Dorrance."

He got up and shook my hand. "Will you send me a bill?"

"It's been paid."

I left. Constance Thayer and I hadn't exchanged as much as a word.

The morning was sun-drenched and already sultry. The air was thick with pollen and smelled heavily of blossoms. It did nothing for my dull headache.

Lieutenant Romero was leaning against the Mercury. Today it was beige poplin, with a red-and-white silk tie on a white shirt and the cocoa straw hat, adjusted at a jaunty angle to allow for the fat bandage on his right ear. I'd heard they'd pulled enough wood-splinters out of it to reconstruct the staircase banister in Proust's basement.

"Your service told me you'd be here," he said. "You look like my ear feels."

"I feel like your ear looks. How's Pollard?"

"Pulling desk duty until his arm heals and hating it. You can't break as many heads from behind a stack of arrest reports."

Pollard had been one of the officers wounded during the fight. "How'd you talk him into coming along on a raid of Proust's house?" I asked.

"At first, of course, we didn't know that's what it would turn out to be. When we got there I promised to shoot him if he didn't go in with us. He believed me. It must have been the hot blood."

"He believed you because you meant it."

"Maybe. I'm not Colonel Seabrook."

"You were at my office early?"

"We were waiting in the empty one next door when Hubert — that was his name? — let himself into the office across the hall. We could've taken him then, but where I was born we wait for the big fish. There was also a question of jurisdiction, not to mention the fact that the only charge we had to hold him on was breaking and entering a vacant office, which we were guilty of ourselves. I put a note on your door for the others when we left to follow. I knew there would be others," he added with a straight face.

"Good thing you waited for them before going in."

"I had disciplinary problems as I said." He took a long cigar out of the lacquer case.

I lit it. "What happens now?"

"Proust has resigned to devote time to his defense. City Prosecutor Fish has appointed Chief of Detectives Frank Knowles to fill in as acting police chief until a permanent chief can be assigned. Knowles is a good policeman by Iroquois Heights standards. You'd have to know him a long time to realize he's crooked."

"You mean deputy chief."

"The chief retired. According to the boys on the third floor, it happened right after he invited Proust to his house and took a typewritten resignation and his service revolver out of his bathrobe and said either Proust's signature or his brains would be on the sheet in five minutes."

I grinned. "It's a good story."

"I wish it were true."

"So who's the new chief of detectives?"

"Not me. The talk is it will be Lieutenant Reuben Zorn."
He saw my face change. "Know him?"

"I knew him when he was a sergeant. I'd have bet then
he'd wind up on charges, but that was before I knew how
bad things were in the Heights. Are you sticking?"

"Someone has to. If I can stay honest I might be chief myself after another few shake-ups."

"I think you will."

"Be chief?"

"Stay honest."

He showed me his white teeth briefly. We shook hands
and got back into our cars.

I drove back to the office. Unlocking my door I said hello
to a sign painter lettering DR. W. W. JOHNSTONE ASTRO-
LOGICAL PROJECTIONS on the door across the hall. I
picked up my mail from under the slot, carried it into the
private office, and dumped it on the desk. I didn't pass any
customers. It was too early for a drink so I filled a glass
from the tap in the water closet and swallowed its contents
in a lump. Then I sat down and called my answering service. One of the messages was from a Mr. Livingood. I
called him.

"Fair shooting up in the Heights." He sounded cheerful.
"I prefer woodcocks myself. More of a challenge."

"I'm glad you showed."

"We wanted him kicking, you know. Care to guess where
he stashed the stuff he took off the fairgrounds? He never
told his grunts."

"It'll turn up."

"That's what I'm afraid of. Well, hell. Plenty more where
that came from, and it beats watching him appeal convic-
tions past the year 2000, although an arrest in this case
would've made me a bureau director. They don't care for
this Dillinger Squad stuff in D.C."

"Did you want to be a bureau director?"

"Hell, no. I never made any secret of the fact I'm just basically treading water till retirement. I just called to say we're even. Sounds like a song, don't it?"

"Thanks. I appreciate it."

"Cheer up. The world's out one asshole."

"Plenty more where he came from," I said.

"Did you expect them all to disappear?"

"I wasn't expecting anything."

"That's the spirit." He hung up.

I looked at Custer. He was still losing. He would always be losing no matter how many times I studied the picture. He looked good doing it, though. I gave him that.